THE HUNTER
AND HER WITCH

Praise for *Freyja's Daughter*

"[Sullivan] builds a rich version of our world with an easily recognizable Seattle setting. With clever wit, she crafts a battle between Wild Women and Hunters that will inspire readers to fight the patriarchy."—*Publishers Weekly*

"A promising debut from Rachel [Sullivan], *Freyja's Daughter* is an immersive urban fantasy novel with a satisfying feminist theme. Minor conflicts and tensions interplay with the main plot to lead the reader to a thrilling denouement. *Freyja's Daughter* is a rare treat for urban fantasy fans."—*Readers' Favorite Book Reviews*

"Ms. [Sullivan] does an amazing job of giving each of these tribes of women (huldras, mermaids, succubae, rusalki, and harpies) different traits and building background. Faline, the main character, is a huldra and a wild one at that! This book is her self-discovery journey. She gets into some trouble, has some adventure, and above all learns what makes her different! I recommend this debut novel from Ms. Pudelek for anyone who loves paranormal romance or even just paranormal at all. I was enraptured from the beginning!!"—*Nerd Girl Official*

"A female bounty hunter with hidden powers and a low lying buzz of chemistry with the cop she interacts with had me pulled in. With an unexpectedly good storyline and a premise that reminds me of authors like Ilona Andrews and Nalini Singh, I was wildly entertained with fantasy creatures walking among us, living for the night, and saving the day. *Freyja's Daughter* has strong female characters, captivating content, and Rachel

By the Author

Freyja's Daughter

Lilith's Children

Ishtar's Legacy

The Hunter and Her Witch

THE HUNTER
AND HER WITCH

by

Rachel Sullivan

2025

THE HUNTER AND HER WITCH
© 2025 BY RACHEL SULLIVAN. ALL RIGHTS RESERVED.

ISBN 13: 978-1-63679-830-1

THIS TRADE PAPERBACK ORIGINAL IS PUBLISHED BY
BOLD STROKES BOOKS, INC.
P.O. BOX 249
VALLEY FALLS, NY 12185

FIRST EDITION: FEBRUARY 2025

CREDITS
EDITOR: RUTH STERNGLANTZ
PRODUCTION DESIGN: STACIA SEAMAN
COVER DESIGN BY INKSPIRAL DESIGN

Acknowledgments

A huge thank you to my readers. Your willingness to swim in the pools of my imagination, making them your own, fills my heart to overflowing. With this book, as well as my others, I hope that you are entertained, encouraged, and empowered.

To the courageous souls who brave their fears to start anew.

CHAPTER ONE

Oriana

Rain drizzled beneath a cloudy March sky, the perfect weather for witchcraft. I grabbed a candle and a lighter from the mantel and headed toward my laundry room, which doubled as a mudroom. After zipping my coat up, I stuffed the glass-encased candle into one pocket and slipped the lighter into the other. For my last order of business, I pulled on my paw print rain boots, a necessity for country-living in Washington State.

The rain boots, not the paw prints. Though the design made them my favorite boots.

I had gifted myself the boots when I first bought this property, before the months of building permits and the well and sewage installation began. Next, I wanted to get a dog to slosh in the puddles and tromp through the woods with me.

One goal at a time. That's how I got through the shocking realization that my whole marriage had been a sham.

One goal at a time is the only way I survived my hellish divorce. It's also how I promised myself I would stay single, by focusing on my list of personal goals.

Cold, moist air swished across my face as I stepped from my back porch onto soggy grass. Every evening I made this trek out my back door and into the relatively unknown. Every evening I explored a different portion of my land. I had walked my whole property before I bought the place, but not in this way, not in a slow search for my tree—the being I'd build an altar around, where I'd meditate and seek centuries of wisdom from a rooted friend.

With my new life came new decisions, and without my own seat at nature's table of guidance, I didn't feel equipped to move forward. Yes, I had bought a house and moved without a wise tree to guide me, but I had other means of counsel: the coven sister, Serene, who I had lived with while waiting for my house to be constructed…my psychic, therapist coven sister.

It was time to lean on my own understanding of the unseen, my specific modality when working with energy.

Less than a year ago, on my thirtieth birthday, I ripped myself from the life I had always known to start a new one.

I also found my first gray hairs, but we don't need to talk about that.

It hadn't been easy by any stretch of the word, but living freely gave me life. I was in a home I had picked, the finishing touches all chosen by me, right down to the earth-toned rock-tile housing today's fire for me to warm up to once I finished my tromp through the woods.

I smiled inwardly at my recent accomplishments. So far I felt at home in my new mountain town of Cedarsprings. The people were friendly, and my coven sisters were closer than family. Now I just needed to find the tree on my property who would give me guidance.

I headed northeast, through the clearing around my home, and into thick woods. Maybe today would be my day. Mist dampened my skin, and I smiled at the scent. Crisp. Clean. I had already tried twice before to introduce myself to who I thought would be my guiding tree. Both times, I hadn't even finished my meditation before the tree let me know we weren't a good match.

Nothing like being rejected by a tree.

Not that the feeling of rejection hadn't become its own fuzzy blanket of familiarity these days.

My first job interview in Cedarsprings was tomorrow morning, and receiving a grounding treatment from a tree bright and early in the morning would bring my interview game to a whole other level of charming professionalism. My coven sisters had offered to employ me part-time to do secretarial and energy healing work for their businesses, but I gratefully turned them down. I wanted to do my own thing. I had lived too many years under the watchful gaze of someone

I had a personal relationship with, and I didn't intend to keep that trend going. So, during the months I had lived with my coven sister and waited for my mobile to be pieced together, I completed a yoga training course.

That was my grand plan to stay independent. I would get a part-time job in town for insurance and a steady paycheck, while building my very own yoga healing practice.

Of course, I hit a snag after I'd gotten settled into my mobile and realized that, as a Washingtonian, practicing yoga outside in the fall, winter, and spring was probably the most foolish idea I had followed through with since getting married. One rainy class of no-shows nixed that whole idea. And it would be a year or more before I could afford to hire a construction crew to build an all-season yoga studio so I could offer indoor classes. My savings had suffered a quick death when I bought this land and home of mine.

Thus, my morning interview with the local school district to fill a paraprofessional job posting at Cedarsprings Elementary School.

I slowed my pace as I neared a grouping of trees. It appeared as though each trunk chose to grow in just the right spot to create a nearly perfect circle of evergreen friends. I stood in the center and spun on my heel, taking in each and every plant being around me. My heart swelled with appreciation for everything. All of it.

Yes, pain and uncertainty and the aftereffects of abuse still hung heavy across my shoulders and forced tears from my eyes at random moments, but what lived around me, what stood before me, were my dreams made reality. And no amount of circumstantial pain could erase that.

My focus narrowed in on a midsized evergreen. I silently walked to the base of its trunk, where I knelt until my knees pressed into the soft, damp, pine needle–covered soil. I pulled the candle and lighter from my jacket pockets and lit the flame to set it between the trunk and me. Closing my eyes, I slowed my mind and absorbed the sounds and shifts in the breeze around me. I exhaled and sank deeper into a state of relaxation.

My brow loosened. My jaw slackened. My breaths grew deeper, longer. I imagined roots growing from beneath me, into the soil. My legs tingled with relaxation and connection to otherworldly things, unseen energies coexisting in the forest.

"This is not your tree," a woman said not so softly from behind me.

My eyes sprang open. In my attempt to jump up and face the intruder, I nearly toppled headfirst into the tree. My candle fell over, snuffing out the flame and spilling drops of melted wax onto wet pine needles.

I spun to face a woman taller than me with a lean build, high cheekbones, and long red hair cascading down her shoulders. I didn't need to slow my mind and focus my energy to feel the power almost vibrating off her. What kind of being was she?

"This tree," the woman said, motioning to the tree I'd gifted with spilled wax, "is young and sickly. She's not your tree."

"I don't mind its age," I argued.

It occurred to me I was disagreeing with a stranger about a tree. Human or not, she was still a stranger on my private property. "And who are you?" I asked, a more important piece of information to gather.

"Whether or not you mind, this tree is in no shape to access wisdom from the roots of the older ones, enough to guide you," the woman answered. "She's busy just trying to get enough nutrients from them to survive. It's been a harsh winter for her." The woman looked past me. Her eyes softened as she regarded the tree, as though she was laying eyes upon a rosy-cheeked child in bed with a cold.

"Who are you?" I repeated, fascinated by how this woman's energy cascaded across her body in much the same way as a deeply rooted tree's. I *saw* her energy as though it was a tangible thing. This woman had swirling energetic branches growing from her shoulders, and roots from her ankles and feet, in a way that seemed to pulse with a symbiotic connection to the nearby plant life.

I placed my hands on my hips and stepped aside enough for her to get a full view of the evergreen I'd just hoped to connect with. "And how do you know so much about the trees here?" I added, which was code for *Why are there energetic branches growing from you?*

Her attention snapped from the tree and landed on me. "I'm huldra," she answered. What looked like tree bark rose from her pores and crawled up her skin, from her wrist to her elbow, as though she was proving her point. As though she was physically confirming my third eye's sight of her treelike energy.

I appreciated the confirmation. Huldra are one of many sects of folkloric women who were created by their Goddess, to have her abilities, many years ago. The huldra were created by Freyja, the succubi by Lilith, the xana by Danu, and the list goes on. All these sects together are called Wild Women.

"I've heard of you," I answered. I didn't add how I'd heard of her kind. They'd basically started an uprising of Wild Women, beings witches had believed didn't exist on this continent. They knew there were groups of Wild Women scattered throughout the world, but they were like the other secret sects of folkloric folks—free and incredibly private.

According to my coven, when the Wild Women in this country began their uprising, my covenmates had felt a stir of energies coming from western Washington, then the whole state, and then the country. A sudden feeling of anxiety, of the unknown thing approaching their reality. Of course, my coven didn't realize there were literal groups of women so oppressed. They were oblivious to the Wild Women's existence in the state until the women burned the whole Hunter establishment to the ground.

If my coven had known, they would have helped.

It was before my time in Cedarsprings, but according to my coven sisters and the coven ghosts, the day the Wild Women burned it all down was one hell of a revealing day.

It was then that my coven learned Hunters, our archenemies, had been operating under their proverbial noses. That the Hunters had traded one mode of oppression—religion—for another more modern way to control Wild Women, through the government. Though their ideals hadn't changed. They still saw themselves as chosen by God to eradicate evil from the world. And what did they deem evil? Any being who opposed their perception of what their God wanted, especially powerful female beings who refused to hand over their unique abilities and livelihoods to be controlled in the name of a male God.

"Huldra," I finally stated when it all started clicking. "Aren't you the women who guard the trees? Listen to them?"

"My name is Faline," she answered. "Faline Frey. And yes, we are guardians of the forests, descendants of the tree women, created by the Goddess Freyja. Our foremothers live in the trunks of the oldest and wisest trees in the world."

Half responses spun in my mind. I muttered an incoherent question that even I didn't fully understand.

The name *Faline* sparked a memory, but not a very strong one. I had heard the uprising began with a Washington huldra, one who'd been stolen from her clan, and another, her sister, who'd led the fight to get her back. Was Faline one of these two huldra?

"I've come to see the new witch of the Obsidian Falls coven, as per my ancestor's direction," Faline said.

"That would be me, Oriana," I answered. "But what can a witch do to help a huldra? Witches use our connection to nature to shift energies enough to make things happen...or not happen. But you're already strongly connected to nature."

Faline shot a gaze to a leafless blackberry bramble tightly woven around and between two trees and gave a quick, short nod.

A toddler with dark auburn hair and round brown eyes ran to Faline and clutched at the huldra's jeans-covered calves. She reached down to pick up the little one and rest her on her right hip. "This is my daughter, Friday," Faline explained. "I was told you need to meet her."

"Told?" I asked, unable to hide my smile from the girl, despite my irritation at her mother feeling it appropriate to enter my land without my permission. Not to mention, I had a tree guide to locate before my interview tomorrow.

"She is the first of her kind," Faline said, stroking her daughter's chubby cheek with nothing less than awe of the pure little being. "There have been Hunter and Wild Woman hybrid children before, although they were created and trained for war..." She looked off into the woods for a moment before settling her gaze back upon her child. "Most were killed, and those who weren't still suffer intense trauma." She sighed and kissed her daughter's head. "Friday's father is a Hunter and Wild Woman hybrid—one of the few who survived. With me being huldra, she is the only Hunter-huldra-xana in existence. I work with plants, but she is potentially able to work with water, sound, and much more than beings with roots. She needs someone able to work with multiple elements and energies at once."

I studied the child closer, the glint of knowing in such a young one's eyes. The green energy of a fully balanced heart chakra emanating from her whole being pulsed with each heartbeat.

She lived love.

Never had I encountered someone who embodied love. And I used to work with children on a daily basis—children are the closest beings we have to those who embody love.

"Xana are connected to pure bodies of water, right?" I asked, making a mental note that I needed to brush up on my Wild Women facts. I knew Danu created them, so I decided I should start by learning more about the Celtic Goddess of nature and wisdom, the mother of the Tuatha Dé Danann people.

Ages ago, the Wild Women and the witches worked together. The Wild Women were a huge umbrella group made up of smaller all-women, folkloric sects who connected physically and energetically to nature. Witches were also a huge group made up of smaller all-women covens who could bend the energy of nature. In fact, when we witches were being called out and burned at the stake by the same people who'd been secretly coming to us for herbal tinctures and blessings, the Wild Women stood at our defense.

They bravely fought by our side, even during many of the Inquisitions.

But when the power-hungry switched tactics and used propaganda to incite fear of witches in the minds of the human masses, there was not a lot left to do but hide. That was back during the last round of Inquisitions. When humans were used as weapons against us, there was nothing we could do but scatter for survival.

From what I had heard, the Wild Women and the witches hadn't communed since.

"Yes," Faline answered, "the xana are connected to pure water and pure love. Their songs can cause the listener's heart to bubble over with either the listener's own good intentions or bad. Bad intentions can kill the person housing them."

Faline gingerly touched her daughter's lips and gave a smile. The huldra's tough exterior cracked open each time she set eyes on her child. "But you haven't found your voice yet, have you?" she said through a smile to her little girl. "And it's a good thing too. Sometimes Mama's intentions aren't so pure."

The little one nervously nuzzled into her mother's chest, uncomfortable with being the center of attention.

So I took the attention and placed it on me.

"How can I help?" I asked.

"You have a unique set of skills," Faline said. "After my ancestor told me to find you, I did a little research."

"I went to school to be a paraeducator," I answered without thinking. "And I'm also a certified yoga instructor. Oh," I added, "and a witch, through both practice and genetics." Because there was a difference.

"You're not just any paraeducator," she said.

I cocked my head in question.

"You work with special-needs children, with a preference for those with behavioral difficulties."

"Yes," I answered, "but I highly doubt a xana would have a tendency toward disrupting class and hurting their peers."

"A huldra and a Hunter would," Faline said with a smirk.

And suddenly it occurred to me, in the way that an aha moment smacks you upside the head and temporarily removes all social politeness from your mind.

"Your ancestors didn't send her to me because she's huldra and Hunter," I said, spilling words from my mouth the moment they came to mind. "They sent her because she'll soon fight a raging battle within her—a battle of light and dark, of good and evil. Much the same way a human child manifests behavioral problems when they struggle to reconcile their light with the horrific darkness they've seen of adults. They must exist in a constant state of conflicting realities. Acting out is how they release the tensions that build up inside on a continual basis."

I thought for a moment as the pieces of my mental puzzle fit into place. "I've seen human children who act out when these types of difficulties swirl inside, and it's not pretty. I can't imagine the destruction a powerful child like Friday could do."

Faline's forehead furrowed as she drew her lips into her mouth.

I had offended her.

But I had also spoken the truth.

So we stood there in the forest, not talking, while she swallowed down her pride and I waited to allow the truth of my words to sink in. I didn't mean them in a negative way, only in an honest way. How she took my truth would determine whether I could work with her in any context.

I gave her a moment.

When her shoulders slackened, I continued.

"Parents tend to think that discussing their child's struggles is picking on their child. And with the wrong person, it can be. But not with me, not with someone who only wants to help children lessen those struggles. But to lessen them, we need to teach them how to cope, and to know how to cope, how to overcome, we need to unearth all the potential pitfalls and the causes for those pitfalls. We need to know *what* they are overcoming to know *how* to do it."

I put my hand in front of me, palm up, and raised a ball of pink light into existence. The energy of healing love hovered above my palm, its varying shades of pink weaving into itself, ever moving. The light, which grew to about the size of an orange, illuminated the darkness around my wrists and forearms with a light pink hue.

Friday turned from her mother's chest to take in the sight, as though she could not only see it, but she could sense it as well. Her huldra mother didn't seem to notice I held anything, but the xana surely did. My chest filled with a new warmth. I couldn't wait to work with this special little girl.

"So then you'll work with her?" Faline asked, her tone serious.

"I will," I said. "It would be my honor."

"And what would you require for payment?" Faline asked. She clearly wasn't sure if she liked me or not, and I really didn't care.

I concentrated on the ball of love energy and thought of different shapes to shift the pink energy's form. A heart, then a pyramid, then an evergreen. Friday smiled.

"No payment necessary," I responded, then thought better of giving my services away for free. I had a huldra asking what she could do for me. "Tell me which tree on my land is my teacher."

"No," she stated, as though I was asking too much. "Your request is for them to answer, not me. It wouldn't be right to speak for them in that way."

"Okay," I said, thinking about the connection between balance and consent, embarrassed I'd suggested such disrespect to my teacher tree. It needed to accept me on its own, in a way I understood. The connection needed to be personal. "I can't think of anything I need… other than a yoga studio. But that's way too much." I refused to take advantage of a woman in need.

"Done," Faline said, turning on her bare heel and heading away from me. Friday rested her cheek on her mother's shoulder and reached for my pink heart-shaped ball of light as she was carried away.

"I'll be in touch," the huldra said as she made her way deeper into the woods, her back to me, before disappearing into the woods, into the night.

CHAPTER TWO

Sarah

"You know," Marcus said, sitting across from me in a cozy four-person booth at the Olive Garden.

Humans would probably call it a large booth, but with two Hunters occupying the space, it seemed cramped. I sat across from him, but if we were side by side, our shoulders would be touching.

Hunters were naturally large—male, female, and everyone in between. Until around a year ago, I had mistakenly thought bigger equaled stronger. They all thought that, because they were all bigger than most others. Even in the supernatural community we were seen as large and in charge.

If you looked at our body styles, instead of the color of our skin and hair, you'd think we were brother and sister. Marcus's lineage was from the popes of Spain, while my father descended from the popes of Germany.

"A new one showed up after last night," Marcus said, rubbing the pads of his fingers over the fresh ink on his forearm, a filled in triangle the size of his fist.

A sleeve of black art had been forming along his skin since he completed puberty and experienced the presence of Wild Women. I was told that when his inner Hunter locked on huldra Faline, now his wife, that's when he noticed the uptick of newly forged permanent markings.

Hunter tattoos created themselves through extreme acts of difficulty and strength. And I was told they were painful as hell, like a hot needle being dragged across your skin. Not that I had ever done anything deserving of a tattoo. Even if I had, though, as a woman I wasn't sure Hunter tattoos were possible.

"It doesn't match," I muttered into my fruity drink, eyeing his arm. Yes, I was slightly jealous that if I wanted a tattoo I had to pay for it and pick it out.

He gave a half laugh. "I know. It's oddly feminine."

I nodded. "What do you make of it?" I asked. Then I thought of a better question. "What caused it?"

Marcus shrugged his broad shoulders, muscles shifting in the movement. The cushion beneath him protested. Most chairs did. Muscle weighed more than fat, and Marcus was pure muscle.

"Was it being your steroid teddy bear self?" I asked, feigning seriousness.

That did the trick. His lips parted in a goofy smile, finishing off with a chuckle.

"I had a dream, after our briefing last night," Marcus confessed in a low tone. "A huge black dog attacked Faline and Friday. I wasn't there to stop it." He took a swig of beer. "I woke up with this triangle and one hell of a headache."

The briefing last night.

During the Witch Hunts, Wild Women—folkloric women created by their Goddesses—protected the witches. That's how they became the enemies of Hunters, supernatural men born to uphold the laws of their God. As the world grasped patriarchy like it was a morsel of—albeit poisoned—bread to starving people, Wild Women fell from their respected roles of healers and protectors among humans. They were turned against, just like the witches.

Over time, the Hunter organization grew, and the Wild Women fell into obscurity, hiding among humans. They were forced to make regular check-ins with their local Hunter authority, their abilities policed and shamed out of them.

Until Faline and her fellow Wild Women flipped the script and burned the Hunter establishment to the ground. It took years for us to actually realize our new reality wasn't a fantasy, smoke and mirrors. And since then, ex-Hunters like me, who wanted to make a difference in the world, met for something we called briefings.

Last night we were told that the uptick in negative entities crossing into our physical plane of existence was rising. That was calm-speak for *Nefarious baddies are crossing over in droves to ruin the lives of humans.*

"You think that black dog in your dream was one of the beings who shouldn't be here?" I asked seriously.

Marcus set his mug on the table but didn't let go of the handle. "I do. And I think the triangle is a symbol of female, but that's all I got." He eyed his new tattoo. "Probably my most shocking tattoo that's shown up since the one that hit me sideways the first time I truly wanted to kill for Faline. The first time my Hunter designated her as my mate."

"Wait. What?" I said, leaning toward Marcus and quieting my voice. "That's a thing?"

Marcus released his mug's handle and leaned his chest across the table to whisper a response. "It's not talked about a lot because when Hunters follow the old ways, they rarely feel a true love they'd kill to protect. Their reason for killing to protect is more about protecting what they own and what's owed to them." He winked and leaned back. "But it exists."

"And so we"—I corrected myself—"male Hunters get special tattoos that just pop up when they kill for love?" It was an awe I felt for my kind that I had never felt before, a kind of magical sense to Hunters. Maybe I was a romantic mush for connecting love to a lifelong unconsented tattoo, but it sounded like something out of a movie or something.

Marcus picked up his beer again and flexed his forearm, shifting the art etched into his skin. "It goes way deeper than killing for love," he added. "In the moment, something bursts inside, and you know there's two possible outcomes. One in which your partner dies, and one in which she lives. You are the pivot point between the two, and nothing but keeping her alive matters." Marcus took a swig. "The blink of a second when every molecule in your Hunter knows you've found your match and nothing will get between the two of you."

The pious religious meanings of the tattoos scattered along on Marcus's arm were in complete contrast to the drink he held, condensation dripping from the cold mug onto the table. Hunter males drank, but not in public, lest they cause another to stumble into addiction. It was a weird rule and one I was happy to see die, along with the establishment itself. Not that it had anything to do with me, a female, one made to sit on the sidelines and cheer the real heroes on.

Faline and her kind would never know the amount of gratitude I held for them, for freeing me. For freeing all of us, really, from the rigid rules that dictated our very existence. And it wasn't as though we had much of a choice but to follow them, when the rules for living were programmed into our heads from childhood and reported to have come directly from the powerful man in the sky who created us all.

As if men could create and sustain life.

"What?" Marcus peered down at his mug as his eyes followed to where I'd been staring, lost in thought. "I assumed you didn't like beer. You want a taste? It's an IPA."

I scrunched my nose at the idea. "Ew, no thanks. Just thinking about how ironic it is that we're sitting here, you chugging a beer, and me sipping a cocktail...in public."

He set his drink down. "According to the Hunter ways, alcohol wouldn't be allowed even to grace your lips, at home or in public."

True.

In my old life, as a woman I wouldn't have been allowed to drink alcohol at all. We were considered too weak-minded, too easily tempted into promiscuity, or whatever other bullcrap they tried to shove down our throats and call medicine. For our better good.

I rolled my eyes at the stupid double standard and where my mind had taken it. "No, not even a drop would touch my wimpy lips," I responded matter-of-factly, "but a strong and probably dangerous pharmaceutical they pretended was a healthy supplement, that one got to take a daily ride through my digestive tract."

"The irony isn't lost on me." Marcus half laughed, half scoffed, reaching for a breadstick.

Funny. In the last year since I'd stopped taking the medication prescribed to all women of Hunter descent, irony had been the theme of my life. Since the Wild Women took down the Hunter establishment and word about the pills had leaked out slowly, along with other unearthed Hunter secrets.

The women's daily dose of goodness had, in fact, been created to suppress our Hunter abilities, those same abilities Hunter males began to exhibit when they hit puberty. Made sense why my father started bringing my pills home from the so-called pharmacy the day I started my period. Some girls' fathers had them begin taking the medication at the first sign of breast growth, or body odor, but mine disagreed with the practice, said it would be easier for me to breed if I waited until my first bleed. Sounded like something you'd say about farm animals, not your daughter.

I still hadn't figured out my father's thought process behind that, but then again, I rarely understood why he did what he did. And looking back, I doubted solid information on the female Hunter anatomy had anything to do with his decision-making.

I'd grown up outside the Washington Hunter complex and had played with Marcus when we were younger. Of course, like any good Hunter family, my father tucked me away in the home with my mother, laden with household duties, once my womanly features began exposing themselves. When I had questioned his new rule of keeping me home, he had responded, "How would you feel if you caused your brother to stumble? You'd have to carry that guilt for the rest of your life. And do you think another Hunter would want you after knowing the evil power you have over men? They wouldn't be able to trust you to birth their sons."

That had shut me right up. Guilt and shame had a way of sealing lips and hardening hearts.

Once the Wild Women toppled the whole Hunter establishment, and their rules were no more, Marcus and I reconnected, old friends who became new friends again. And when the truth came out about the medication, he had urged me to quit taking it, implored me to accept my strength.

Yeah, at the time, that was a hard pass.

It took me years and three therapists who specialized in spiritual abuse and cult deprogramming before I even considered stopping, before I felt capable of seeing my true self…the way I was made to be.

A female Hunter. A lesbian female Hunter.

Which was Marcus's newest point of peer pressure—for me to start dating.

"I'm telling you," he went on, circling back to his earlier topic, "plenty of succubi would be more than happy to date you, show you the ropes maybe. No strings attached even, if that's your thing." He winked.

I accidently let out a nervous half laugh and shook my head. "I don't even know what my *thing* is. And plus, I'm pretty sure it doesn't work like that."

"At this rate, it's never going to work like anything." He raised his dark eyebrows. "I'm just saying."

"Hey," I said nervously, still thinking about our Hunter talk. "What did it feel like when you first encountered your Hunter?"

"When it first took over?" he asked.

I had never heard of it like that, taking over. I had always connected it to puberty in a sense and figured a male's Hunter came on like that too—step-by-step. "There's a single moment when it just takes over?" I asked, perplexed and interested.

"You can feel hints of it here and there, but yeah, there's a moment when it arrives with a bang and kind of knocks you on your ass." He leaned back and stretched his shoulders, as though his body was remembering the feeling. "It's different for everyone. One guy told me he completely blacked out for hours. Woke up like he'd been on a bender or something. In training they told us these wild stories of how the old saints' Hunters arrived. You know, the Hunters who were eventually sainted."

I nodded. As a girl I had never been privy to the training Marcus referred to, but I had always been intensely curious.

"Yeah, they said those guys went a little nuts. But they were the most powerful too, which is why the establishment sainted them as vessels for the original saints." He looked over his shoulder to watch his wife approach us. "That's old Hunter lore, though," he added, smiling in his mate's direction.

Faline made her way around a corner painted to look like stucco or some sort of old Italian bistro wall and heaved a purse onto the table. "You guys are lucky this place is full of humans who can't hear your conversation." Friday perched contentedly on Faline's hip. They only played the toddler-on-the-hip facade around outsiders. Otherwise, the girl clung to the back of one of her parents, her legs wrapped around a waist and her arms around shoulders.

Nonhumans must learn to fit in to the human world even before they can walk.

"Marcus," Faline said in exasperation, "stop trying to fix her up. She'll find someone when she's ready."

Friday reached for her dad, who gladly accepted the little one into his barrel chest and then scooted in toward the faux-stucco wall so Faline could sit beside them.

"Don't mess with the succubi," Faline warned me, taking a sip of her mate's brew.

"Why?" Marcus asked, not breaking eye contact with Friday, who traced her dad's lips with a tiny, pudgy finger. "The succubi are good people."

Faline bit a chunk from a breadstick and talked around her food. Apparently, manners were no match for hunger. "Because"—she swallowed and took another bite—"her heart will get all tangled up."

"And falling in love is a bad thing, because…?" Marcus asked, a hint of teasing to his voice.

Faline groaned. "She just shouldn't fall in love with the first woman she sleeps with. She needs to find herself romantically, what kind of women she prefers, what kind of romantic interactions best suit her."

"And dating a succubus can help," Marcus argued.

The two were sitting there discussing my sexual life like they knew. I didn't know crap about it, so yeah, I was listening.

"If her first sexual experience is with a succubus, she'll fall in love," Faline warned, leveling her gaze at Marcus and then switching to me for some reason. Clearly, I wasn't a part of the conversation, so I had no idea why she peered at me.

"I'm not huldra," I reminded them. "I wasn't born with a natural rejection of all things romantic love and coupledom."

"Neither was she," Marcus said the moment I finished.

Faline shot him a questioning look but couldn't ask what he'd meant because the waitress showed up at our booth, placed our meals on a folding table, and asked if we wanted cheese grated onto our food.

Friday crawled underneath the table and back up the bench on my side to sit beside me, where her spaghetti had been placed, with plenty of added cheese on top.

"Explain," Faline demanded of her husband once the waitress left our table.

Marcus swallowed his mouthful of meat lover's pasta with a playful grin, clearly getting satisfaction from irritating his mate. "You were oppressed by the Hunters, so it's only natural that your kind would want to do the opposite of what they did. Hunters married in their twenties, and usually not for love but for procreation and an imbalanced facade of a partnership. So huldra chose a very different route—never fall in love, never marry, only have one child for the sake of keeping the species alive."

Faline seemed to lose interest in the topic and shook her head, engrossed in the plate of food in front of her, pasta with steak pieces. "You're wrong," was all she said before waving the discussion away and starting her meal.

Marcus shrugged. "I could be." He took a swig of beer. "So, how'd today go?"

"Mmm." Faline grabbed the cloth napkin from her lap to wipe sauce from her lips. "Good. She'll do it. And for a small price too."

"What's that?" I asked.

"The witch in the Obsidian Falls coven," Faline answered. "She'll mentor Friday, and in return we'll build her an outdoor yoga studio fit to use year-round."

"Year-round in Washington?" I asked with more scoff than I'd meant. Washington state and rain went hand in hand. Outdoor yoga in all weather sounded illogical and muddy.

Neither Faline nor Marcus seemed to notice my lack of enthusiasm.

"Mm-hmm." Faline gave a nod. "And I know just where the yoga studio should go. All I need now are volunteers to construct the thing."

Six months ago, I held a hammer for the first time. It felt wrong, holding a man's tool, doing a man's job. But soon enough I found myself seeking out reasons to use my newfound strength to pound nails into wood. Feeling the Hunter blood course through me was one thing, the power that almost mimicked a panic attack. But releasing it, that was more than cathartic—it was enlightening, like seeing myself firsthand, the way I was made to be.

And it turned out, I had a knack for building.

"I'm in," I offered.

"What about your job?" Marcus asked. "Aren't you guys finishing up with that home development build?"

"Meh," I said. "My part is pretty much done, so I can take vacation until we get a new contract." Rarely had I found myself with opportunities to help Faline and Marcus, after they'd helped me so much. When one showed itself, I jumped on it. If I got to swing a hammer in the process? Even better.

"Okay." Faline picked up her fork, preparing to get back to her meal. "We need to draw up the plans and then order the wood."

"We should ask the succubi what the perfect yoga structure should look like," Marcus suggested. "Especially if the witch teaches kundalini yoga. That's right up their alley."

"Good idea," Faline responded. "Once we can get a date for when the lumber will be dropped off, we'll know when to head over to Cedarsprings. Get a few more Hunter-born to come with for help." As though she'd had enough of that topic, Faline settled into the booth's cushioned bench and started making quick work of her meal.

As I sipped the rest of my soup, a single thought played through my mind. More like a new fear brimming to the surface. Witches. Real, powerful witches. How would they react to me, the lowest of the low? A female Hunter.

CHAPTER THREE

Oriana

In the early morning hours on my first day of my new job, I sat beside my newly built firepit and watched the flames dance against the repurposed bricks Serene had dropped off a couple days before. They were left over from the haul she'd gathered from a demolished old building outside of town, and they worked perfectly at keeping the fire in place.

Every little accomplishment I made on my personal to-do list gave me more than a sense of satisfaction. It symbolized another weight lifted. The fire was no exception.

No amount of staring at the fire, though, could answer the big question on my mind at the moment, the most pressing matter of all.

What did I want my yoga studio to look like?

Important stuff. Important enough for an early morning phone planning session.

"You'll definitely need walls, so you can teach classes in the winter," my Seattle-based yoga teacher and friend, Raven, suggested over the phone.

"Yeah," I answered, transfixed by the flames. I sat on the single stump I had dragged over to my firepit. One day there would be a circle of stumps around the old bricks. "I was thinking thick canvas walls that I can remove in the summer and warmer spring and fall days, for the views."

"Perfect," my very hippie friend replied. "Once you get set up, if you ever want to host a retreat there, I know of a bunch of folks who would love a weekend in the mountains among like-minded people."

I smiled.

Yeah, I guess my coven and I could be considered like-minded to those who sought to better themselves with mindfulness. Of course, the witch part of my identity never entered our conversations, and it never would. She assumed I was like her, and in some ways, I was.

"That's a great idea," I replied, with no intention to follow through. A regular class of local residents was one thing. A large group of expectant out-of-towners tromping through my woods had no place in my vision for the future.

Sure, Ostara was coming, our spring holiday celebrating new beginnings, and I had already invited my coven over to my property for its first ritual. But it would only be my coven who practiced any sort of magical work in my woods.

Bringing a group of strangers to the small, private town of Cedarsprings would be a mistake for a plethora of reasons, the biggest being the pissed-off witch spirits who popped up in the most random places without warning to terrorize newcomers into leaving.

I didn't blame them, though.

They had deserved respect as the granddaughters of the founders of our town. What they got was the wrong side of a noose. The newcomers they'd encountered in life were focused on land for the taking, and eradicating the coven of witches in their way. The fact that these women's grandmothers, who'd founded Cedarsprings, also happened to be queer, unmarried ex-harlots who practiced witchcraft hadn't helped their cause.

My phone buzzed with an incoming call, so without thinking, in an effort to end the current topic of a retreat from progressing to making actual plans, I quickly told Raven I had another call and switched the line.

"I'm not doing so well," the male voice said, nearly in tears.

My stomach twisted at the sound of his voice. Stupid. I was so stupid for answering without checking first.

He didn't wait for me to reply…or hang up on him.

"I lost my job, Oriana. After working my fingers to the bone for them for five years, they just fired me, like that, for no reason," my ex-husband, Steven, whined.

"I told you to leave me alone," I answered. "You were probably drunk at work again," I scoffed. "That's a pretty damn good reason to fire you."

Shit. Why did I engage him? I scolded myself.

Every time.

Every. Fucking. Time.

Before I could right my wrong, he pleaded, "I have nothing left to live for."

I rolled my eyes. I'd heard that one before, a couple hundred times.

"I swear, I haven't been drinking," he added. Ah, another classic.

"Oriana?" His voice was slightly back to normal, getting the hint I wasn't falling for his whining. "Without you, I have nothing. I mean it this time." He quieted, waiting for my reaction.

The first few times he had insisted he would consider my wants and needs now that he realized he couldn't go on without me, I did everything in my power to meet him halfway, to change the one thing about me that kept us from being together, so that I could help him love me the way he claimed to want to. I had even put my own career and health on the back burner. Now his empty promises just pissed me off, the fact that he was willing to play ping-pong with my emotions and didn't think twice about it.

Steven thought way too highly of himself to embrace any long-term changes for the good of our relationship. He seemed to think how he lived and functioned was perfect—I was the imperfect piece in the puzzle that was us. I used to feel bad even considering a reality in which he only said and did things to benefit himself, but my coven sister and licensed therapist Serene had assured me countless times that this was a textbook strategy to ensnare me into feeding his ego and allowing the mistreatment to continue. He wanted a reaction from me, a glimmer of hope on my end, to show I still cared about him. It didn't matter whether the reaction hurt me in the process.

"I told you, Steven, I'm not riding your roller coaster anymore," I said dryly.

"You're such a manipulative bitch!"

Ah yes, now for the aggression portion of his manipulation strategy.

"You used me, just waited to make enough money to leave me. You only wanted my money, and now look what you did. I'm unemployed because of you." Serene had referred to this portion of Steven's tactics as self-projection: He's too perfect to cause any of his own issues, so they must be my fault.

And that was my cue.

His rant continued—more about how I used spells to wreck his life—as I pulled the phone from my face and pressed the red *End* button.

I made a mental note to sage myself before leaving today. I had made strides in my healing where Steven was concerned, but his voice and manipulation still put me on edge in an awful way. Sage smoke had a way of delighting my senses and calming my soul.

I stood from my tree stump and stirred the remaining fire to snuff out the flames until only red embers littered the bottom of the pit. Finishing the last swig of coffee, I headed into my mudroom to remove my rain boots.

The scent of freshly brewed coffee still filled my house, despite the pot being empty. I passed through the kitchen, made sure the red coffeepot had turned off automatically, and made my way to my bathroom to shower.

Hot water pulsed from my showerhead, billowing steam over the sliding glass doors, beckoning me to step inside.

Warmth cascaded down my hair and smothered the crisp chill still lingering on my skin from the early morning air.

"I rinse off any belief or energy that is not naturally mine," I stated, imagining the grime of manipulation sliding from my skin.

As toxic as Steven was, and other people like him were, it had to come from somewhere. People couldn't be born without the ability to experience empathy. From my many sleepless nights of reading, trying to wrap my head around how someone who claimed to love you could hurt you so badly, I gleaned a little understanding. The strongest theory for why people lose their ability to empathize has to do with a traumatic childhood in which either one or both parents were emotionally distant and emotionally abusive. It didn't excuse Steven's behavior, but it did help me remind myself not to take his words personally. His opinions and thoughts were more about him than me.

It also made me want to help others, particularly young children from abusive backgrounds who could use a little empathy and care.

I smiled, steam encasing me in comfort. A year ago, it would have taken me much longer to calm the inner panic Steven had a way of setting off. This morning, though, I was using what I had experienced and learned for good. It was my first day of working with the children of Cedarsprings Elementary, and I couldn't feel more ready.

❖

After the workday I'd just had, exhaustion weighed down on me like a suffocating blanket. I slipped my Converse from my feet, kicked them away from the walkway, and shut the front door behind me. I trudged five steps to my thrift store couch and gave up on standing.

"Tell them to leave!" a feminine voice commanded.

I sprang from the couch and caught the shadow of a woman wearing a long dress, standing in the darkness of my hallway. I'd encountered the witches of Cedarsprings's past, during rituals with my coven sisters, but never alone in my house.

It was so unnerving that the hairs on the back of my neck tingled.

"Who?" I asked, fully awake now, my blood pulsing though my veins like race cars on a speedway.

"The others, they will bring attention to the falls," she moaned.

"Our coven is safe," I assured the dead witch.

What I thought was a dress billowed out to reveal itself as a dark hooded cape, exposing a white dress beneath. She wore her hair long, and it shifted unnaturally, as though electric energy wove through her tresses despite the gentle flow of her garments.

"Our kind isn't hunted anymore," I said. We didn't go around announcing our existence and showcasing our abilities to outsiders, but there weren't hooded men scouring the towns for us either.

In a blink she hovered before me, the lines on her face visible, her sneer of disbelief undeniable. "*Never* assume you are safe," she bellowed. "Such assumptions lead only to death."

My pulse slowed, and I took a cleansing breath, compassion replacing fear. Odds were, her life had been riddled with threats to our kind and ended in a hanging or a burning. Many of the old Obsidian Falls coven had shared such a fate. Our foremothers came to this remote place to live their authentic lives in peace with nature. And nature responded with nutrient-rich crops, which eventually caught the attention of outsiders looking to settle such a wild terrain.

"Okay," I said as I backed away from the spirit and sat on the couch. I grabbed my phone from the purse I'd flung onto the plush arm only moments earlier. "I'll call the coven about it, and we can decide from there."

When it came to town matters, just like our ancestors before us, we always made the decisions as a coven.

"No need," she replied, less end of days and more irritated with my naivety. "You summoned them—you tell them to leave."

"Wait." I put my phone down on the cushion beside me. "Are you talking about the huldra? She's back already?"

It had only been a couple weeks since her first visit when we arranged our agreement. I still hadn't figured out my plans for the yoga studio. Not to mention, the spring weather of rain-soaked days followed by colder, rain-soaked nights wasn't exactly conducive to building a wooden structure on dirt in the middle of the woods. I had figured they would wait for drier weather.

A new panic set in.

Did she expect me to have the area cleared? Hell, did she expect me to know where to build the thing? I had an idea, but I hadn't fully settled on it. That would take time and mulling over.

"Stop your worrying of petty nuisances," the witch interrupted.

She appeared natural and yet unnatural at the same time, standing in my living room.

From her cloak and dress, I'd say she lived in the mid to late 1800s.

"Your energy is spinning out of control. It's making me tense." She placed her hands on her hips and gazed out the wall of windows to my left. "I am dead. I have nothing to be tense over."

Dusk covered the property, and a question popped into my mind, distracting me from my worry. "Can you see in the dark?" I asked.

She shot a questioning glance to me. Her tone sharpened when she said, "Honey, I *am* the dark."

She had a point. Still, it didn't answer my question. I thought better than to ask again, though. When the dead refuse to answer a question, no amount of asking will make them spill. It only frustrates them. And to piss off a dead person would be a mistake.

"If it's the huldra," I said, back on topic, "she's no danger to us. She's here to build something for me because I agreed to work with her daughter."

She let out a low, unnerving laugh that seemed to vibrate through the air. "Fine, then. I will assist you in this." She shook her head as though I was putting her out with my request.

People complain about the complexities of communicating with those in older generations, how they don't seem to be speaking the same language. Try dealing with personalities from generations back.

"Assist me with what, exactly?" I asked.

She sighed, the sound carrying itself into my bones. "The little girl is a witch. She will need an instructor."

Now it was my turn to laugh. "I'm also a witch and could instruct her if she was a witch, but she's not. She's Hunter, huldra, and xana, an already unprecedented combination." One that I didn't have the first clue how to handle. I'd barely researched these creatures on their own, let alone meditated for wisdom on the sensitivities, weaknesses, and abilities the combination created.

The dead woman looked toward the back side of my house, my bedroom. "They are here. And you are wrong, young witch. It is not only huldra kind waiting for you."

Before I could ask what she meant and remind her I was in my early thirties, not young, she vanished.

A knock sounded at my door.

I got the distinct feeling that not only had the dead witch been right, but she had failed to mention the huldra had brought others with her—dark, oppressive, dominant beings. Their presence weighed down the energy around my home to a low dull vibration.

Negative entities were attracted to low vibrational energy.

Great. Now I'd have a child to teach lessons I had no idea about, a yoga studio to build that I hadn't solidified plans for, and malevolent spirits drawn to my property.

I quickly breathed to root my energy into the earth beneath my trailer and pull up from the soil a protection energy to use as a shield.

Here goes…something.

With as much confidence and energetic protection as I could muster, I opened my front door.

CHAPTER FOUR

Sarah

God, I hoped she didn't have her coven with her. More witches meant a better chance I would be found out. Could they sense Hunters? I bet they could.

I looked around at the handful of Hunters in front of me, between the witch's front porch and myself. Tall men, none under six and a half feet, with wide barrel chests and forearms the size of a human man's biceps. Some wore jean work jackets, for the wet Pacific Northwest weather, while others stood in the evening's drizzle with only work jeans and T-shirts. Because we felt temperature, but we also ran hot, the men more than me.

None of them seemed nervous. Like they'd just shown up for any other construction project. Did they know we were building on the property of a witch? And if they did, had they considered that our ancestors began a genocide on theirs? By their whole vibe, they were resigned to a day of work and eager to get it started.

Not me.

My stomach twisted.

If I could help my chosen family get in and out, get the job done, without getting myself noticed by the witch or her coven, I would call this trip a win. Tell my nervous system that, though, and my mind, spinning with all the ways my grandfathers could have made the lives of the witch's grandmothers absolute hell.

Mature evergreens towered above us, their branches heavy with rainwater. I stood under one, back at the rear of the group, closer to the vehicles, watching Faline's and Marcus's every move. A fat droplet hit my forehead, but I only wiped it off and continued staring. Faline and Marcus stood on the small wooden porch off a rectangular mobile home and knocked at the witch's front door.

My heart raced for them, which made no sense. Faline had already met the witch, and besides, Faline was a Wild Woman. And Marcus was the son of a Wild Woman, a xana, beings known to be brimming with pure love and the mighty power of water.

They were probably considered allies of the witches.

I was not. I had no mother, no grandmother or great-grandmother who embodied my beliefs and ideals on life, who I could find pride in and through whom I could get a sense of belonging to my bloodline.

I tried to focus my thoughts on other things and studied the mobile home. The witch did have a nice place, though. Her double-wide looked new enough to not include a patch of grass or anything resembling a front yard, only the porch, treated two-by-fours nailed together in the simplest pattern to get the job done, enough to get out of the mud and to the front door.

I made a mental note to let the owner know—if during the build we happened to make introductions—that treated wood still needed protection from the wet weather of the Pacific Northwest. A coat of white outdoor paint would protect the wood and match the trimming on her home.

I wondered where the nearest hardware store was in town but quickly reminded myself the owner was a witch. She wasn't going to shoot the breeze with me or ask about other projects we could do while we were here. This wasn't a normal job with a normal client.

I took in my surroundings. If I practiced magic, I supposed this would be the perfect place to do it, so close to nature and far from people. Her home sat on a small cleared portion of her property, the rest covered by great evergreens and tall, wispy alders. Smoke plumes rose from the chimney. A witch living in the woods. Only this one's cabin was upgraded to cozy, new manufactured home.

Faline stepped back from knocking on the white front door, and Marcus stood on the step below her, waiting. Friday's whispers from the tree line caught my attention, and I smiled, my momentary anxiety relieved by watching the little girl press the palm of her hand against an evergreen and giggle as though the tree just shared its favorite joke.

Often, since Friday's birth, I found myself contemplating what could have been. What *would* have been. How, if the Hunters were never overthrown by the Wild Women standing up and saying *No more!* to their oppression, I'd probably have a little one nearly her age at my feet. And another one on the way.

I had never actually wanted kids, even when my only future in sight included marrying a Hunter male. Back then, I had figured I would have kids regardless of what I wanted—probably at least one boy. How many girls I birthed wouldn't have mattered much. I would have just kept popping out girls until I got a boy. Unless I got a boy first. Those were the lucky women. They weren't forced to turn their bodies into birthing machines, to the detriment of their own health, until their uteruses dropped out or they bled to death.

Escaping that fate sealed me with a lifelong debt to the Wild Women, although Faline and the others disagreed. I was completely comfortable with such a debt. I saw it was a win-win. When it came to the Wild Women, whatever I gave always came back to me with their added appreciation.

They maintained that they had toppled the Hunter establishment for their own freedom from oppression. And that's all fine and well. Why they did it doesn't keep me up at night. Queer and nonconforming Hunters were freed in the process. To me, that's what matters.

Friday pressed her ear to the bark of the tree before her smile dropped. She seemed to listen carefully. She nodded, the side of her face still up against her new friend.

The door to the mobile home eased open, and I swung my gaze to recenter my focus on the scene in front of me as Faline took another step back to give the door room to open. Marcus didn't move from the porch step below Faline. He only balanced himself as her back pressed into him.

The witch's honey-brown eyes struck me, as the porchlight illuminated her from above. She wasn't even looking at me—her eyes seemed to bore through my being with a sense of knowing, a sense of power. The pulse in my neck thudded loud enough for me to hear. I wanted to look away, to escape the intensity I felt, the physiological reaction I found myself caught up in.

Her dark hair hung in a low ponytail, wisps flying around her face, as though to accentuate her wild nature the way a fern extended itself to the world around it in no particular fashion other than its own. It struck me that I had never compared a woman to a plant before. But then again, maybe I had never met a woman to inspire the comparison.

In relation to the doorway, the witch appeared tall and lean... definitely a practitioner of yoga. She wore fitted jeans and a hoodie sweater. Relaxed. I liked that.

I caught my thoughts. Why did it matter that she reminded me of a fern, or what she wore and my opinion of her style? Why did the wildness of her hair make any kind of difference to me? I was there for Faline and Marcus. I'd help them follow through with their agreement with the witch and then be on my way back home to the room I rented in their home. Back to earning money by building homes alongside my ex-Hunter brothers.

It was in that moment, when I stopped admiring the witch, that I noticed the shock on her face—her wide eyes, the way she bit her bottom lip as she took in the crowd of ten, mostly Hunters. Huge men in Carhartt and work boots, strapped with hammers at their waists.

I hadn't considered how we looked from her perch. Until now.

She cleared her throat and focused back on Faline. "No Hunters," she stated, loud enough for us to hear the seriousness, along with a slight shake, in her voice. "My ancestors will not allow these males near Obsidian Falls."

Faline turned and shot a quick glance to me. Friday, Faline, her sister Shawna, and I were the only females in the bunch. I expected Faline to argue with the witch, explain how these males, these ex-Hunters, posed no threat to the local coven or the Obsidian Falls.

Instead, Faline gave a nod. "I understand."

Now it was my turn to be shocked.

Faline reached a hand behind her back to squeeze Marcus's. "This will extend the time period for the project," she warned.

"I am well aware," the witch answered.

For all her beauty and fierceness, any person who hated my kind also hated me. Hadn't she known what had become of us Hunters? Hadn't she heard of those who left the establishment before it fell? Those who helped the Wild Women bring down their own brothers, their own families? Could she even imagine the anguish, turning your back on the only way of life you knew?

I had never fit in with my kind growing up. I felt like a continual outcast. But they were still my family. I still loved them. I still had to feel the weight of their disappointment as I turned my back on everything they believed in, everything they wanted for me.

I did it for freedom. Not just freedom for me—freedom for myself had been an afterthought—but freedom for the Wild Women, for those oppressed by the Hunter establishment, past, present, and future. I knew leaving couldn't fix what had already been done. But I did it to make sure such atrocities didn't continue, my way of stopping the familial cycle.

Each one of my brothers who stood beside and in front of me on this dreary, wet evening had fought for freedom like I had, even to the detriment of everything they loved. Each made that most difficult and self-sacrificial decision. We each continued to struggle with that decision, years after making it.

And each of us had volunteered to help today, knowing it was a witch's property.

This was her show of appreciation? To banish us from her sight, from her property and her town? As though we were not good enough to build a damn yoga studio for her? For free?

I started to walk toward the truck and trailer closest to me, the one loaded with pretreated wood, nails, stain, and hammers. I'd unload it all in the mud for her. Let her build the damn thing herself.

Four Hunters joined me, and as though we were all thinking the same thing, we swung open the back trailer doors to unload the materials inside. No way were we paying the added gas to transport this crap back home. Let her coven figure out how to deal with it.

"Sarah," Faline called from the porch.

I poked my head out from inside the enclosed white trailer, not wanting to actually make an effort to move my whole self. I had a job to do so I could follow the precious witch's orders and go home.

"Will you stay to help Shawna and me construct Oriana's yoga studio?"

Crap.

The eagerness in Faline's eyes revealed a part of her I had never seen before. Desperation. What was this witch supposed to teach Friday that was so necessary? I caught my thoughts. It was not my job to judge the training of Friday. Hell, I could only relate to a third of the child's hereditary abilities and needs, if that. How could I also have any idea of what kind of help or training she'd need? Friday was special, that much was obvious.

And Faline was trustworthy. That much she'd proven, time and time again. Plus, I owed her. Faline is the Wild Woman who started the revolution against the American Hunter establishment. I would always owe her.

I didn't want to, but I jumped out of the trailer with a sigh loud enough for the witch to hear, whether or not she had human hearing. "I'll do it," I answered, making sure my irritation came through loud and clear.

For the first time that I could tell, the witch noticed me. She stared directly at me. Her eyes caught mine, and even though I tried not to read into her expression, I found fear in her gaze. Worry.

She knew I was a Hunter. She feared me. And despite how much my pride wanted to rage at her ignorance for my kind, a rawness buried within me leaked hurt onto my anger, boring holes of uncertainty into it, enough to expose those hidden pieces of myself not even I dared to look at.

With her focus on me, I felt like Swiss cheese, exposed. And not in the good way.

She knew I was evil at my core. It was written all over her amazing face.

God, I needed to get this over with and get the hell home. Before this whole thing turned into an even bigger crap show.

Chapter Five

Oriana

I'd expected Faline to argue with me, so when she accepted my condition of no Hunters on my property, I wondered if she needed me more than she had let on. What was so wrong with her daughter? What was so urgent? I shot a quick glance at Friday, who happily petted an evergreen. One of the same evergreens I had tried to seek guidance from and that had refused to work with me.

I scanned the group of ten or more people standing in the mud, where my front yard and driveway would one day be. All looked ready to begin working, despite the time of day and the lack of light. They wore work boots, gloves, jeans. Some wore tool belts fitted with hammers hanging at their hips. As innocent and helpful as they appeared, I felt the energy they emanated.

I stood by my decision. No Hunters allowed.

In the whole group, I counted two Wild Women besides Faline and Friday. I assumed they were both huldra, though the one standing at the back didn't feel as grounded as Faline and the other woman. She was among those who wore a tool belt, a black-handled hammer resting against her Carhartts, as though she was a Wild Woman more comfortable among Hunters. I saw nothing natural about that.

I had planned to pitch in with the construction of my yoga studio, but now I had no choice but to help. With only four of us to get the thing built, I needed to settle on a more simplistic design.

Faline asked the woman in the back if she'd stay to help, after she had vanished into the trailer they had brought. *Sarah.* I had never heard of a Wild Woman being named after a biblical character. But then again, I didn't know much about Wild Women.

"Do you have a place to stay?" I asked Faline, trying to soften my voice after declaring the majority of the group must leave moments before. The man behind her didn't budge, despite the other men leaving the group to walk back to their trucks.

"We checked in at the town's motel already," she answered. "But it looks like we'll be changing those reservations."

Wild Women and witches went back. Way back. When patriarchy got its foothold into the many cultures worldwide, wise women, or witches, went from trusted healers and seers to evil monstrosities. Books suggesting our kind were better dead than alive circulated and picked up notoriety. The Wild Women stood in our defense, sometimes warning us to flee our homes and villages before the noose came calling, and other times to fight in our stead. They offered a different type of sisterhood to witches. And we've not forgotten their loyalty. Not even the old Obsidian Falls coven witch spirits could argue that.

"Please, I have two spare rooms with beds," I suggested, softening my voice further. "You and your sisters can stay with me. I'd hate to put you out more than I already have."

Faline looked to another woman, Shawna, she had called her, who nodded.

"Okay," Faline said. "But not tonight. We have a twenty-four-hour cancelation clause on our rooms." She turned to the man behind her. "Plus, I'd like to spend the night with my husband before he leaves for home."

Her husband. He didn't feel like the others, but he certainly looked like them. Tall, muscular, tattooed with what I only assumed were Hunter sigils since all the men wore similar markings on their arms. The tattoo that stood out the most to me was the black cross extending along the insides of their forearms. The symbol gave me chills, no doubt the last thing many of my foremothers saw during their torturous deaths.

Why on earth would a Wild Woman marry a Hunter?

"So then," I said, "we'll begin building tomorrow?"

"We had planned to start tonight," she responded. "But due to this newest turn of events, I think tomorrow is the better choice."

I gave an understanding nod. The old part of me, the pleasing-others part, wanted to feel bad, tell her never mind, the Hunters could stay. But I couldn't deny the heavy energy the Hunters brought with them.

It was impossible to please everybody, I reminded myself. *Trying to please them all will only leave me empty and not pleased.*

It was a saying my therapist had taught me. That and *The opinions of others about me have nothing to do with me.*

I clung to these two sayings, burned them into my memory as a go-to for conquering my own self-sabotage.

"I understand," I said, then thought to add, "I assume you'll need a rough design of the yoga studio by the morning."

She seemed to consider it for a moment. "I'd brought one, a rounded design, but given the lack of hands and the fact that I've never been trained in building, I think we should throw that idea out and go with a four-walled studio. Out of the three of us"—she motioned to the other two women who stood nowhere near each other—"only Sarah is skilled in carpentry. I think she'd appreciate if we didn't put more on her shoulders than we already have."

Sarah stood beside an open truck door, as though she was impatient to jump inside. I eyed Sarah's shoulders. They seemed strong and capable to me. Her stoic face held no expression. Even the longer tresses above her freshly cut fade seemed to stay perfectly still in the evening's spring breeze.

I focused back on Faline. "All right then," I said, ready to put this night's awkward encounter behind me and light a joint to smoke my woes away. "I'll figure out a simple design tonight and email it to you before I head to bed." Design first, weed later.

"That won't be necessary," Sarah called out, still standing beside the open driver's side door of the blue truck. "I'll handle it."

Her tone did little to hide her frustration, and the last part was said as though she spat the words at me. What did she have to be mad about? Was she married to one of the Hunters too? I hadn't noticed her standing particularly close to any of the men during her time on my property.

The odd Wild Woman jumped into the driver's seat of the blue truck and roared it to life. She expertly turned the thing around in my circular clearing of a driveway, not allowing even one evergreen branch to swipe across the white trailer. Once turned around, the blue truck flew down the hill of my driveway toward town. Ignitions fired from the other trucks filled with Hunters.

I nearly apologized to Faline as she followed her husband down my porch steps and gathered their daughter. But I stopped myself. Goddess, just when I thought I had healed an aspect of myself, another deeper layer of scars showed itself. Oh well, thus was the lifelong healing journey of the witch.

Instead of apologizing, I kept the door open, watching as the little family joined Shawna in an SUV and left my property. I didn't want to seem even more rude by shutting my door before they were securely in their car.

I half expected the dead witch to be standing in my hall or sitting on my couch when I closed my front door and walked to the dish cabinet along the wall in my kitchen and dining room area.

Nope. She had insisted I kick the Hunters off my property, which I didn't disagree with, suggested I needed help training a hybrid child, told me to never assume my safety, and then vanished.

Yup, that sounded about right. I rolled my eyes.

"It's so comforting to know my coven ancestors are here for me. *So* supportive," I said sarcastically and immediately regretted the attitude behind my words. My coven ancestors owed me nothing. They had already done enough to change my life for the better.

My antique curio cabinet held one row of old scrying bowls and small cauldrons. The other two glass shelves held bottles of wine, including the empty bottles I didn't have the heart to recycle because their labels were works of art. But the real use for my cabinet hid underneath, behind the wooden doors at the bottom of the piece. I pulled open the middle door and removed a red plastic Folgers canister. Grabbing my jacket and boots from the mudroom on the way, I headed down my back porch steps and opened a folding chair to face the dark woods. I balanced the Folgers container on my lap as I pried the lid open and pulled out its contents.

"It's an indica night," I said to the woods. Lacking the patience to roll a joint, as I had previously planned, or even to grind the leaf, I stuffed a nugget of plant into the bowl of the dark pipe and lit the end.

A crow landed on a lower branch of a bare alderwood at the edge of the woods. A layer of mist crawled across the damp night air to hover slightly below the crow's perch. If not for the moonlight, I wouldn't be able to see the black bird.

Soon, the alderwood would begin sprouting bright green leaves to go with its lean beige and white trunk. I couldn't wait to see my property in each and every season of beauty. Couldn't wait to sit out here at nine o'clock at night in the summer and it still be light.

The crow cawed at me to make sure I knew of its presence.

"I see you," I assured the animal. "Have you come to bring me a message?"

It only stared at me. Unlike what you'd read on the internet, animals and plants do not each have one singular representation. Crows symbolize different things to different people. Animals, plants, and stones are directly connected to nature, the way humans once were. In their connection, the animals have a better sense of energy flow. And in energy flow we find spirits and deities, the power of the winds, and the knowing of all that ever was. So to say that each animal represents one thing, based on one tradition, is ludicrous.

The world is too vast and too old for that.

The crow's presence reminded me of the Morrigan, Celtic Goddess, one of the group of deities believed by the Celts to have founded Ireland, the Tuatha Dé Danann, and one of the most misunderstood deities. Though, to be fair, the roles of most ancient Goddesses were incredibly misrepresented. People today have a hard time believing women of the past were seen any differently than women today—as anything other than those who tended the hearth, produced offspring, or constantly waged war with an untamed volatile inner nature.

Whether the Morrigan was real or not, I didn't really care. It was her energy I relied on, the energy of battle and war. But not the type of war humans preferred. That was a patriarchal notion. The war she aided in was much more difficult than those fought on the battlefield. She led a person through the daily battles fought within themselves—the process of putting to death those lies fortified by trauma many of us carry in the depths of our souls, where even *we* fear to tread. That is the bloodier war. The most difficult fight, requiring a level of bravery few wish to access.

I breathed out a mouthful of smoke. It dissipated up into the night air. "A new battle is coming, huh?" I asked the crow.

It cawed in return.

I could have guessed as much. "It's the little girl, isn't it?"

The crow only looked away.

"Yeah." I sighed, releasing another billow of earthy smoke. "What do I have to offer a child so powerful, though?"

Other than experience? I sensed my inner self answer. I liked to believe it was my soul responding when this happened, my higher self stepping in to set me straight by stating something I wouldn't have thought of.

I remembered what Faline had mentioned, about her ancestors directing her to me. Why I had connected so well to children with behavioral issues. I understood and respected the battle within, the fight between that which no longer served me and that which is what I've always known. Basically, the fight between the parts of me placed there by trauma, and the parts of me I was born with. Did little Friday also have that tug-of-war playing out behind her whispers and giggles and hugs? Not the trauma part; I wasn't assuming her young life included abuse. But her blood did include two enemy species within one being.

The crow cawed, and I found myself studying it. "I have something for you," I said, setting down my Folgers container and gently placing the pipe on top. "Be right back."

I rushed into my pantry and grabbed a rosemary cracker, normally saved for special nights with wine and goat cheese. I slowed when I stepped back onto the earth, careful not to scare my new friend away. I passed my plastic folding chair and crept to the alderwood, holding the cracker out away from my body and up toward the lowest branch. Mist swirled around my wrist as my movement broke through the horizonal haze.

"Thank you, new friend," I whispered to the crow. "Thank you for reminding me what I'm capable of."

The beautiful onyx-feathered creature jumped from its perch, grabbed the cracker from my outstretched arm, and flew away with the offering.

It never failed. When life felt overwhelmingly impossible, nature had a way of bringing it all into perspective.

I finished smoking the leaf and emptied the ash into the moist dirt beneath me, tamping it down with my boot's sole to make sure it was out. "Thank you, Goddess," I said to the Morrigan. "Thank you for teaching me to fight."

I considered my next week or so, getting to know the child and whatever difficulties Faline had been so urgent to get help for. I would soon be navigating an environment in which Wild Women lived in my home. I had no idea what all that meant, making emotionally preparing for it more than a little difficult.

Of course, this had to come at me all at the same time, hosting Wild Women houseguests while placating a dead witch who demanded obedience, deserved respect, and insisted on helping me with Friday. All while starting a new job with troubled human children to care for on a daily basis.

"Goddess," I pleaded, "make me ready for this upcoming inner battle. Please, don't let it break me."

CHAPTER SIX

Sarah

I waited until the trucks and SUVs full of Hunter males pulled away from the hotel parking lot, leaving a single extended-cab dually hooked to the trailer, before venturing to Faline's room. I had figured she would want to spend time with Marcus as a family before they parted.

Gray skies knelt to the ground, leaving the parking lot in a sweet-smelling mist.

"Come in," she said after I knocked on her green motel room door. Her and Friday's things had already been packed up, and the room looked ready to vacate. I nearly offered to take their bags down but remembered she was huldra. A huldra who had been using her abilities for a while now, so she was practiced in them. She was stronger than me.

"You've eaten, right?" she asked, setting Friday on the edge of the queen-sized bed and maneuvering little green frog rain boots onto her feet.

"Yeah." I shut the door behind me. "The others and I went to a breakfast diner here in town before they hit the road. I'm stuffed." I patted my stomach.

"Good." She smiled. "And how do you feel about sleeping at the witch's house tonight? I should have asked you and Shawna first, before agreeing to it. If you want to stay here instead, I'll understand completely."

I did want to stay at the hotel. But there was no way I was leaving Faline and Friday and Shawna alone. I might be female, but I was still a

Hunter, naturally skilled in the protection of others against supernatural beings, especially the protection of those I love.

"No," I answered in a breezy way, like wherever I slept was no big deal either way, "it's okay. I want to stay where you guys are staying." Faline finished with Friday's rain boots and stood. Friday jumped from the bed and stomped around as though she'd gotten an upgrade in feet.

"But you'd prefer not?" Faline asked, leveling a gaze at me.

"She hates Hunters," I said. "I'm a Hunter." It wasn't rocket science.

"She assumes you're a Wild Woman," Faline countered. "Most have no idea females can embody Hunter abilities. Hell, you all didn't know until recently."

"Yeah," I said, considering that maybe she didn't know what I really was. "But she's a witch, she'll figure it out eventually. And when she does?"

"She'll be busy with Friday. Hopefully she won't be around you long enough to notice you aren't one of us." Faline grabbed a tote bag and the room key card.

Aren't one of us. The words hit a nerve I wished didn't exist. How many times would I hear that phrase in my lifetime? If I truly thought about it, which I preferred not to most of the time, I belonged to no group. Not specifically, anyhow. I belonged to no one and nothing.

Leaving the Hunter lifestyle was like tearing my skin from my muscles and examining the rawness and pain left behind. What hurt? Why did it hurt? What did it mean in regard to who I am? Having to completely question everything you thought you knew, including your own self, was not a fun or pleasant process. It was the reason most female Hunters made the decision to remain in the dark about who they really were, what they were really capable of. Some began the process of stopping the meds and quickly realized it was more than they were willing to risk.

I never faulted them.

But I also found it harder and harder to relate to them. Not to mention the whole lesbian aspect. Whether Hunter women liked it or not, they were raised in fear of those who were different. And I'm different.

Out of all the beings I hung with on a regular basis—or, I should say, spent time around—Shawna and I got along the best. We were both supernatural beings, both female, and both attracted to women. Except she was a Wild Woman, with her incredibly tight-knit band of Wilds, and I wasn't.

Even among those who were different, I was more so.

I brushed Faline's *one of us* comment off and held the door open as she grabbed Friday's sparkly pink overnight bag and gave the room a once-over. Friday's pudgy hand fit into mine as we walked down the stairs to the truck. After a quick text from Faline, Shawna came out from the motel's office and hopped into the front seat of the truck, beside me.

My anxiety grew as Faline buckled Friday into her seat behind me. I started up the truck and made my way out of town and up the mountain road leading to woods and witches. Leading to one witch in particular. The Hunter hater.

I parked the loaded-down truck in the witch's muddy driveway and told myself that if this thing got stuck in the mud, trapping me with the witch, I'd have no qualms rolling up my sleeves and pushing the thing to freedom. Doing some Hunter stuff. Right in front of her gorgeous, judgmental brown eyes.

"You ready for this?" Shawna asked, clearly intuiting my discomfort, something she seemed to do often.

I pulled the key from the ignition and gave a heavy sigh in response.

"Yeah," she said with a smile, staring ahead, "if my ancestor hadn't insisted on bringing Friday to this woman, I wouldn't be here. I can't stand bigots."

"Bigot?" I asked. Kind of a strong word.

She nodded. "What would you call a person who generalizes and dismisses a whole group of people?"

Hunters were bigots, though I wouldn't count myself among them. So hearing Shawna call the witch that jarred me a little. It had taken me a while to fully accept that I came from a lineage of hate. To wrap my understanding around another version of the same kind of hate…my head wasn't ready. I was still unpacking what it looked like in my own upbringing.

I leaned my head back onto the headrest of the driver's seat. "Everything is so damn confusing lately."

"Change usually is," Shawna countered from beside me. "Doesn't mean it's bad, though."

I straightened my spine and turned to look into her chestnut-brown eyes. She wore her black hair in braids, all gathered into a ponytail today. Normally she kept them down, so I assumed she intended to keep them out of her face for the manual labor today would bring.

Shawna had a way of blowing me away by her mere presence—her wisdom only added to my thankfulness to know her. She had gone through so much, and at the hands of Hunters, no less. And yet through it all she gained a wealth of strength and knowing I rarely saw in a person. When we had first met, I had thought to pursue her romantically. But we quickly realized our chemistry was one of friendship and not eros. Even that, being open to me despite my affiliation with her captors and abusers, made me respect her more if that was possible.

"I think you should lean in to your confusion," Shawna added, gathering her purse from the truck floor beside the center console. "Too many people run away from it and never get to totally understand where it stems from. Roots of confusion are usually just new understandings waiting to be unearthed."

She shrugged as though her words weren't packed with layers of truth and depth and grabbed her cell from her purse. "Signal up here is shit." Then, as though an afterthought, Shawna added, "Try cussing in front of the witch. Hunter women don't cuss."

"I cuss," I countered, pretending to be offended. And I hardly looked the part of a Hunter's wife, meek and mild.

"No, you don't," Shawna responded. "*Crap* and *hell* aren't cuss words."

"What?" I said, exasperated. "I'm not used to saying them. So they are to me."

Faline unbuckled Friday. "Well, now that we've gotten *those* facts out of the way, we should head in before Oriana thinks we're waiting for her to leave, or talking about her. No sense in making things more awkward than they're already going to be."

By the time we all had boots on the ground, Oriana stood at the top of her porch, her front door open. "Welcome!" she called out, in a very nonbigoted way. I scolded myself for defending her, even if just in my mind. Bigots don't have a way of sounding. "Let me grab my boots and meet you out back. You can come in through the mudroom."

The front door shut. I paused, waiting for the Wild Women to move while I still watched our surroundings. When Faline and Shawna began heading for the back porch, I dropped my gaze from the northern tree line and walked beside them.

As we squished through the muddy, turned-up soil of a plot freshly dug for the placement of a new mobile, I became more aware of what this witch's lack of acceptance was costing us. Basically, our whole crew. Instead of ten sets of hands building the yoga studio, there'd now be three. Three sets of hands. Another reality set in.

Crap.

That meant we'd be here longer than originally planned. I didn't have much to go back to, but the idea of staying up here on this mountain—with a witch who hated my kind—for any more time than anticipated pissed me off. My footfalls sank deeper into the mud with each step. God help me.

Oriana

Had there only been three grown Wild Women in the bunch? Had I ever stopped to count before declaring Hunters were not allowed on my property? I closed my front door and rested my head on the square panels. A deep sigh left my lips. Three. There were three Wild Women here to build my yoga studio. How the hell was this going to work?

I opened my eyes to see my new resident witch spirit, the tip of her nose nearly touching mine. I startled, which did nothing to move her.

"Not right now," I said with way more disrespect than I meant. I moved past her and shook my head. "I'm sorry, that was rude." Before throwing the back door open, I thought to add more. She deserved more. "Anywhere I am, you are welcome." And I meant it.

She gave an acknowledging nod.

I plastered a smile on my face and opened the door to greet my visitors. Screw it, so I'd have to help them build my yoga studio. In the elements of early spring, in western Washington, when I was probably the only being in the group who felt temperature.

Life happened. What were you gonna do?

"Welcome, welcome," I said to the Wild Women in my friendliest thank-you voice. My covenmates would roll their eyes and call me fake if they heard me right now. Although I would disagree. It's called kindness.

Faline waved a hello while the one with braids glared at me and Sarah watched the woods around my house. Something about her caused my eyes to linger on her longer than the others. Yeah, she looked a little out of place—not as femme, I guessed, as the others. But there was a certain appeal I couldn't put my finger on. I'd dated women before, so I wasn't confused by my attraction to her. But there was more than a physical lust playing in my body. There was something I'd never felt.

I tucked the thought away to examine at another time and waited for Faline to get within six feet of me, tromping up the back porch steps, before I backed away to give them all space to enter. Friday clung happily on her mother's back, clearly interested in her new surroundings. As much as I loved my new laundry room, complete with a mudroom sink, it didn't fit all of us. I turned to lead them down the hallway to their rooms before Sarah, the largest of the three adult Wild Women, crossed the threshold from the porch.

I wondered what kind of Wild she was. From what I'd seen and heard, the huldra were leaner and lankier. She didn't look like a huldra. I pivoted to my resident spirit for a quick mind reading and answer to my question, but she was gone.

"Is something wrong?" Faline asked, halfway down the hall when I pivoted to stare right at the empty wall.

"No," I stuttered. "I just…" I searched for a logical response. "I just really need to put some art on these walls. They're bare."

They weren't. Just that one was.

They peered around at my walls, and especially back toward the living room, which was full of plants and candles and…art.

As if I hadn't realized how ridiculous I looked, I pushed open the door to my spare room and pointed to the queen bed sitting in the center, a colorful patchwork quilt draped over the top. "Faline, you and Friday can sleep here," I said. I tried to make eye contact with the other two, but only the one with braids looked back at me. The other seemed to study Faline's room.

"I'm sorry," I said, hoping to draw Sarah's attention enough to start a conversation. "I don't know your names."

Her green eyes flashed to mine with an intensity that took my breath away. Power sat calmly inside her like a lion, patient and waiting. I blinked to release my connection to her inner self. Did she notice I had fibbed about not knowing all their names?

Thankfully, she responded right away, saving me from my own awkwardness.

"I'm Sarah," she said, cocking her head at me as though she felt my intrusion on her inner self and wondered why I'd been so open with my abilities to a stranger.

Or maybe I was just assuming that.

"My name is Shawna," the other woman answered. I turned to look at her as though the act was an afterthought.

I was botching this up, and I hadn't even gotten to the bad news. I let the words fall from my mouth because there was no good way of saying it. "I have no beds for you, Shawna and Sarah. I'm sorry. The other room is supposed to be my office, but I don't even have a desk yet."

Buying more furniture than I started with required a job. An income. And with only a few days of my new job under my belt before spring break, my measly paycheck wouldn't cut it.

"That's fine," Sarah said, shrugging her shoulders. Everything about her tone and the relaxed expression in her eyes told me she really was fine with it. Huh. "Shawna, you can share the bed with Faline and Friday. I'll take the couch."

"Here"—Faline rolled up the quilt that had been lying on the bed and threw it to Sarah—"we don't need this."

Sarah stood frozen, her eyes wide and focused on Faline.

Faline cleared her throat.

"I know you don't need it either," she stammered, "but we have a bed, you deserve the comfort of a blanket." She paused. "To lie on."

"Okay," I said, keeping from them the fact that I'm a witch who reads energy. And lying—or anyone who doesn't actually believe what they're saying—puts off an energy of fear and uncertainty. If I told them, they'd stop. I preferred to know the lie rather than have them not say anything at all. "Well, you can leave your bags in here." I opened the door to my empty, furniture-free office. "Free up more space in the bedroom."

I looked to Sarah to let her know that offer extended to her as well, when I saw them.

Muddy boot prints.

On my new carpet.

Tracking all the way down the hall.

My expression must have been intense because all three of them looked for whatever I was staring at. I lifted my gaze slightly to examine their shoes. Faline and Shawna barely had any dirt on their shoes, as though they'd glided across the mud out back.

Sarah.

My eyes traveled up her body. I didn't mean to, it just happened.

And before I knew it, before I could hide my frustration and absolute annoyance, Sarah spoke to those exact feelings.

"Crap, that was me, sorry," she said, relaxed even in her apology for tracking mud all over my house. My new house. "I'll clean it up. Like it never happened."

I nodded, unable to say anything productive. I wasn't usually this type A, but the boot tracks triggered me—something deep and painful and rooted into my brain. The way heartache and pain tended to clamp on to your emotions and seep their toxicity in, until those memories controlled how you felt about things. About everything.

I needed to step outside. "I have to...I'll be right back," I said, preparing to push past the women huddled in the hall. Instead, they pressed their backs against the walls and cleared a path for me.

Cool March air greeted me. I inhaled deeply through my nose, imagining fire moving down my throat, filling my lungs, and filling each cell of my body, from the top of my head to the tips of my toes. I exhaled, imagining flames exiting my body through my mouth, taking with them the burned pieces of fears and beliefs that no longer served me. Those things clinging to my mind, my thoughts, my emotions moments earlier were now a smoke tendril in the wind.

My pulse slowed with each breath.

In. Out. In. Out. In. Out.

The release of pressure built up by those things which do not serve me. They had at one time served me well, those fears of being belittled for caring that the floor not be filled with mud, holding back my request that he take his shoes off if they were dirty because I knew from experience that my wants didn't matter. Not to him.

And deep within that fear lived a pulsing hurt.

The hurt of a reality in which the person you love more than anyone else only cares about you in as much as it affects them.

That's what kept the fear in place, glued it down despite the hours on top of hours of meditation and hypnotherapy and energy healing. You can't safely and fully release fear while the hurt still thrives. And an emotion like hurt deserves respect, to work its way out in its own time.

So I kept to stealing away when the fear rose up and pounded through my heart. Breathing cleansing breaths. Rooting my energy to the soil beneath me, no matter how many layers of flooring or deck stood between us. Each time, I prayed to the Goddess, asking her to help heal my hurt. To help me be ready to let go of the fear. And each time I was reminded to accept the pace at which my body, mind, and soul chose to heal as the perfect pace for me, the right timing.

My elbows leaned on the porch railing, my back loosening as I gave a hard exhale. I returned to my normal breathing and used the moment to thank the Goddess, to appreciate the nature around me. Handling a panic attack came much easier in nature than it did when I lived in the suburbs.

"Thank you," I whispered into the breeze and turned to return to my guests.

The back door swung open, inward, and I nearly walked right into Sarah. Another inch and we would have been touching.

What was with the beings getting in my bubble today?

Sarah froze. She only moved enough to bend her neck to look down at me. I looked up at her. The automatic need to move back never entered my mind, until I realized it hadn't entered my mind.

"I really am sorry," Sarah said, this time with concern in her voice. Her dark eyebrows drew together. "If I can't get it clean myself, I'll pay a professional to do it. But either way, the mark on your carpet will be gone soon."

The warmth of her body radiated. The V at the base of her throat, exposed by the V-neck T-shirt she wore, called my gaze to linger, dared me to look a little lower.

I felt that power again, but this time it moved within her, not in a rush or even a jolt, just smooth waves. The waves comforted me, lulled my anxiety with a promise I knew I could trust.

"Okay," I said, my face relaxing into a smile. "That means a lot." Not the words, but the energy behind the words permeated me with a knowing.

Everything in me demanded I touch her, that I share my energy with her. I took a risk and went with my feelings. I placed the palm of my hand on her stomach to show my thankfulness.

Sarah jumped back, her eyes wide with confusion.

And maybe something else.

Ah yes, I knew that look too well.

I dropped my gaze from her and left her alone on the back porch. Going against every bit of gracious hosting within me, I walked through my kitchen, past the Wild Women who also didn't give two shits about me or my feelings.

I had read Sarah all wrong. Because more than her energy, I knew that look. It had been burned into my corneas after years of gazing upon it.

I had shoved past them all to be alone in my room. In my house. The one I bought for myself. Where I could live alone for the rest of my days and be completely happy. Goddess knew, I'd rather be alone than have to see that expression pointed at me ever again by someone I thought I liked romantically.

Yeah, I didn't need to read energy to know the look Sarah gave me, what really lived in her mind when she conjured thoughts of me or, in this case, when I touched her.

Absolute and utter disgust.

CHAPTER SEVEN

Sarah

I stood in the forest, the full moon hanging low and heavy in the dark sky. It didn't take much time surveying my surroundings to come to two conclusions. One: I'd never been in these woods—magic pulsed through the trees, dripped like raindrops from the ferns. Two: These woods were not safe.

My Hunter senses felt it, warned me.

And yet I kept my boots firmly in place.

I peered down at my boots. Black. I didn't own a pair of black boots, and for good reason, which showed itself as my gaze climbed my own body. Black cargo pants and a black long-sleeve shirt. I wore the Hunter's garb, our uniform—at least the one my brothers, cousins, father, and grandfathers wore while serving the Ultimate Purity.

It was their, or should I say *our* way of excusing the harm done while in the uniform. A uniform replicating the black cloak of our ancestors, the black cloak of the executioner for whichever king ruled in whatever region at the time. There were too many kings, too many regions, too many generations to count.

My ancestors had always served those in power and called it divine purpose.

Black-colored garb kept the blood of witches and Wild Women and other heretics from showing, from staining.

Once, when I was little, I had asked my father an innocent question. "Father, why do you not wear the color of purity in your work?"

My child mind just knew my father was good and did the heavenly work of ridding the world of impurities, the way one would cut the bruise off an otherwise perfect apple. No one mourns for the bruise or cares that the bruised part of the apple had no choice in what trauma had caused the unsightly portion in the first place. We cut it off and throw it away. No thoughts given. That's how my people operated. So as a child, to ask about purity in uniform made sense.

It also made my father smile.

He rested his big, calloused hand on my shoulder with warmth and leaned down with a sparkle in his eyes. I had just known he was about to share a secret with me, some lesser-known Hunter fact I could run off to my friends with, and whisper the tale in their ears.

At that age I still played with the Hunter boys. We hadn't hit puberty and been completely separated yet. It was rare that I or one of the other girls was privy to Hunter tidbits. Hunter boys were doted upon and groomed from birth, given enough information to make them excited to grow up and fight alongside their fathers. So when I got the opportunity to dangle a juicy truth over the boys' heads, one they didn't already have stored away inside them, I jumped at the chance.

"You ask a great question, Sarah," my father had whispered in response. "What we do day in and day out is pure, God's work, indeed."

Pride had welled within me. My chest, full and warm, swelled. I was the daughter of a great Hunter, and he said I asked a great question. My smile had outshined his in that moment. I had been sure of it.

"But, my girl," he had continued, "what we men fight is not pure. She is twisted and evil, so much so that she doesn't know her place in the world—she believes herself to be on top, above us."

I nodded. My father did not only refer to the Wild Women believing themselves to be above Hunters, but any females who believed themselves above males. This was not only an affront to nature, but an affront to God himself. He created women to be helpmates to men. And those who refused to submit to this natural way of things were cast out, like Lilith, who had been created alongside Adam but refused to lie under him.

My father had stood, his chest wide, his arms strong and thick, his many tattoos hidden underneath black sleeves. He straightened his pants and the ornate leather belt his dagger hung from, safely in its sheath.

He had patted me on the head. "What we must fight, what we must know, is not for your kind and innocent mind to worry about. These things don't belong in the minds of women, who already struggle with impurities."

He sighed and gave a chuckle when I opened my mouth to remind him I wasn't a woman, as though I was defending myself, as though I was reminding him I'm not one of them.

Not yet.

I was still good, still his little girl. I hadn't come into my evilness yet. My breasts had not begun to bloom.

"One day," he had said, leaving me to move toward the side table beside the front door where his keys and wallet rested in a blue flower-shaped glass bowl. "Sooner than you think, you too will begin the process of changing." He placed his hand on the doorknob and turned it, revealing the outside. I didn't move to hug him good-bye. Especially not with the door open, in full view of other Hunters living on the compound, walking the grounds in all black.

My father had stood outside now, ready to close the door, to temporarily cut me off from the outside. "And once your body changes, your mind will go too, twisting our ways in all manner of directions, mostly to suit your fleeting hormonal wants or desires. I wouldn't want to burden your mind with things it cannot decipher correctly." His gaze moved past me to the opening to the kitchen. "One day you'll begin your medicine, daughter, and it will help keep your evil at bay."

And with that, he shut the front door.

I never brought up the question of their uniform color again. Somehow my child self knew two very interwoven truths. One: Hunters dealt with the darkest creatures of all. And two: As a future woman, I was one slipup away from that darkness, one wrong thought from wildness.

From my blood belonging on my father's uniform.

And so, I stood, an adult woman, in a witch's forest that oozed magical energy—the kind that pulsed and spun just out of sight—wearing a Hunter uniform. A uniform I'd never been allowed to wear and then had decided I'd never wanted to wear.

But somehow, after over a year of consciously making sure to never pair my black shirts with my black pants, I'd done just that. I blamed the slipup on my preoccupied mind and told myself to just not think about it.

I reached to touch the tip of a fern, drooping with droplets accentuating the bright green of new growth. I half expected the magic to zap me like a Taser.

It didn't.

As though it was flowing water and my hand a riverway, the magic flowed into me.

As though it belonged.

As though I too was meant to be wild, to be free, like magic.

The soft sound of a door opening pulled me from my dream, but I didn't stir to show I was awake.

So the black uniform, the magical fern, had been a dream.

Oriana tiptoed past me and the couch I half slept on. Gauging the softness of her steps, there was no way she wore shoes. Maybe socks? More likely she was barefoot.

Her scent of patchouli and lavender wafted by me as I kept my eyes shut and my breathing slow and steady, pretending to sleep. I wondered, what kind of Wild Woman did she assume I was that I didn't have extra sensitive hearing or other highly tuned senses to know she sneaked about her home.

Or maybe she didn't care. It was her home, after all.

I tried to keep my business to myself, tried to force myself back to sleep once she crept from her home and out into the darkness of early morning.

Oriana was a witch who hated Hunters, hated me.

Yet I couldn't fight the urge to follow her.

Into the darkness. Maybe it was the realness of the dream that pushed me off the couch and outside. Maybe something completely different.

Did Hunters do this? Had my brothers or uncles or father ever sought that which was not for them? The oil to their water?

Marcus had.

But Marcus wasn't full Hunter.

I was. Pure as they came.

I shook my head. I didn't have to seek Oriana to follow her. I could just be curious.

I wore socks because one blanket on a couch in the middle of March in western Washington wasn't nearly enough to keep me warm at night. But I hadn't asked for more because I was supposed to be a Wild Woman.

I didn't mess with removing the socks or throwing a jacket over the sweater I wore. If a witch could withstand the elements, so could a Hunter.

As I closed the front door silently behind me, I realized the error of my thinking. Witches were one with the elements. Hunters…not so much. Either way, I couldn't turn back. I'd chosen to exit from the front door, so I could sneak around back without her hearing or seeing me.

Dead pine needles and broken branches poked at the soles of my feet. The chill of nearly freezing earth seeped through the stretchy fabric of my socks and pierced my toes. Still, I moved like a cat around the mobile home, clinging to the edges of the building. A branch snapped to my left, past the first line of evergreens into the more wooded area on the outskirts of the cleared space around the mobile. Of what would one day become Oriana's yard.

Without a thought, I followed the sound, moving through the woods from the trunk of one tree to the next, until I spotted the witch in a small clearing, her hands raised to the cloudy sky, rain falling on her face.

My eyes fixed on Oriana. Her pastel nightgown shone in the small slivers of moonlight each time a cloud cleared a path. Her raised arms, thin and dainty, looked to have the power to hold up the sky.

I watched for minutes upon minutes, as her hands stayed fixed above her, as though she was accepting offerings from beyond the sky, beyond the heavens, from a place far more powerful.

I'd seen acts of strength before, strong men dressed in all black, ordained by their God and their ancestors. But hiding behind the trunk of an evergreen, I witnessed something greater that I couldn't quite fathom. A quiet strength, a private one, that somehow rang in my mind as a purer strength, as something stronger and more real than any outward showings of public ritual or the flex of a huge, tattooed muscle.

As the minutes passed, rain saturated Oriana's nightgown, and the fabric clung to her curves. Her hair dripped with water. My thoughts shifted from awe of her power to an awe of her form, the two observances weaving together.

She bent slowly and picked up a jar I hadn't noticed had been at her bare feet. She raised the clear container to the sky and whispered to the heavens, "Thank you Goddess, for your many gifts, for guiding me to this place. I ask now that you sanctify this soil I stand upon. That in this spot, you continue to heal me, my heart, and help me to bring others along this self-healing journey, to help hold space to heal themselves."

She bent again, this time spinning the top of the jar until the lid fell off and onto the moist forest floor. She poured the jar's thick and slow-moving contents onto the earth beneath her. "I give this offering to you, Goddess, to the beings who reside in these woods, those seen and unseen. I thank you and appreciate your presence in this place."

She stood, bringing the lid and the jar up with her, spun the lid securely onto the top of the jar, waited a breath, and turned to head back to the house.

I pivoted to press my back against the tree I hid behind and took in a gulp of air as she passed. When she reached the clearing behind her home, I silently crept to the spot she'd been. Curiosity fueled me, yeah, but also a desire to know this witch. What caused her to remove herself from the comfort of her bed in the early morning hours? What spell had she cast? What liquid had she used to cast it?

I quickly closed the gap between where I hid and where she had stood and knelt to examine her ritual substance. I dipped the tips of my fingers into the still warm thick liquid and brought the scent to my nose. In less than a breath, my curiosity turned to fear.

I wiped the substance from my skin, back onto the earth. Pine needles replaced the spell-casting liquid. I fought the urge to tromp into the witch's home, shove past her, and wash my hands thoroughly with soap and scalding hot water.

My stomach turned as I stood and backed away from the ritual site. Away from the fresh blood.

My interest in Oriana, my growing desire to know her more, hit me like a boney fist of stark reality to my cheek. What was I doing following a witch into the woods, wishing to know her secrets?

It wasn't my desire to know her that worried me, that formed an ache in the pit of my stomach I couldn't ignore but didn't want to banish, either. The Hunter in me could have simply wanted to know more about my surroundings, whose house I slept in.

No, that wasn't what fueled my curiosity for the witch.

It was something else. Something deeper.

Something that scared the crap out of me.

I hadn't loved another woman, and I certainly didn't think I loved this witch. I hardly knew her. I had desired others. Not many, but there had been a couple women that had caught my attention since leaving the Hunter life.

I'd acted on none of my desire.

Yet here I stood, in this witch's woods, remnants of her blood on my fingers.

I had just witnessed blood magic. Her blood magic.

Fear, deep and rooted into my being, rose within me.

This was evil, blood magic. Nothing good came from using blood to get what you wanted.

This witch, Oriana, who'd caught my attention in more ways than one, was truly evil.

I kept my line of sight on the back porch, where I last heard her move. Now her movement was silent if she moved at all. I hadn't heard the back door open or shut, which meant she still occupied the outdoors with me. This witch who poured her own blood as an offering to the Goddess she served.

"I know you saw." Oriana's voice sang to me, from where, I couldn't be sure. "Saw what I did."

I moved out of hiding and toward her voice. I stepped into the clearing of her back yard. She stood on the first step of her small porch at the back of her house.

I paused. Neither of us moved.

We locked eyes. She did not smile, and neither did I. I couldn't guess my expression—was it shock or fear? But she wore one of indifference.

It struck me in the gut. I'd seen that look on my father's face, my brothers' faces. After I'd begun growing breasts, and especially after my first menstrual bleed.

"You should know better." Oriana exhaled. The power she had worn like a crown earlier in the woods was now gone, and exhaustion filled its place. She turned to the back door and shook her head. "What kind of Wild Woman barges in on a woman's ritual, on her private prayers?"

She moved up her porch steps and stood in her mudroom with the back door still open. She spoke out to the night, to me as I waited at the tree line, warring against the rejection and anger swirling through my mind and stiffening my body.

"No Wild Woman I've ever heard of." She sighed and shut the back door, shut me out.

I had not yet spent a day in the witch's home and already she suspected what I knew to be true: I didn't belong. How long would it take her to realize there was a reason she felt off around me, a reason she shook her head at me and sighed in indifference. That soon her sighs and head shaking would morph into screaming and commanding I leave her land, her town.

How long would it take for the witch to realize I was a Hunter?

CHAPTER EIGHT

Oriana

"Joshua in Mrs. Elsworth's class is having a meltdown," Janice, Cedarsprings Elementary School's secretary, said as she lowered the phone onto its holder on her desk. She sat behind the front desk, surrounded by mementoes from her years of life—family photos and a mini Seahawks helmet, probably a gift from a student, knowing her.

If there had been a parent in the office, the break room door would be shut, and Janice would have gotten up to deliver the message personally, rather than calling me from across the room. I think she preferred this way.

I stood from the break room table in the adjoining room and answered through the open door. "Okay, thanks."

Break time over.

Joshua had become a quick favorite of mine. Hell, all my naughty kids were my favorites, each with their own set of talents and whip-smart personalities. Tall for his age, blond haired, brown eyed, Joshua was the only child in Mrs. Elsworth's class who I worked with. There were three kindergarten classes in Cedarsprings Elementary, and I worked with one child in each of two classes, and three in the third, Mrs. Box's class. That poor teacher. She saw me more than the others. I sat among the children on her story time carpet more than any of the other classes.

Mrs. Elsworth stood at the front of her class, instructing the kindergarteners on how to fill in a circle halfway, preparing them for the concept of pie charts. Fresh little faces watched her with big eyes, absorbing knowledge and probably her fantastic coloring skills as well.

I stood in the entrance and searched for my boy. The odds of finding him in his chair would be long. I peered at his assigned seat at a low-to-the-ground kidney-shaped table and spotted a crayon on his empty seat. A math worksheet lay on the floor beneath the table, torn and crumpled.

Meltdown indeed.

Each of my kids had their own response to stress triggers. Joshua's was distracting the other kids, which Mrs. Elsworth did *not* delight in.

There he sat, behind all the tables, in the opposite corner of the room on the story time carpet, holding two wooden blocks together, waiting for the most opportune time to bang them into one another.

Like I said, whip-smart.

If something is stressing you out, what do you do? Change that something. Distract the others. Pound blocks together until the teacher chases you around the room to get you to stop. Anything to take away the bad feelings.

This is why I was brought in to work at this school. I don't chase. Not kindergarteners. Not anybody.

When Joshua noticed my presence, his gaze shifted from his teacher to me. A huge grin lifted the sides of his lips.

Game. On.

I knew his first reaction would be to—

A toy car soared through the air and landed within feet of his classmate, who gasped and yelled his name to scold him.

Oh yes, he liked that. His grin grew. Attention was always a good thing.

Still, I stood, noticing he hadn't yet given up on the blocks now squished together in a one-handed grip.

The adorable little Joshua bounced up from the colorful carpet and bolted for the cubbies.

Despite what it looked like, the young one wasn't hiding in fear. Kids who hide in fear don't wear silly ear-to-ear grins. No, Joshua had switched tactics the moment he noticed me. Distraction time was over. Game time had begun.

I intuited that he didn't have a lot of game time with adults in his home. At school there were adults everywhere, the perfect opportunity to get that need met.

When I didn't respond to his little game of catch me if you can, Joshua began throwing other students' items from their cubbies as he maneuvered a way to fit his whole self in one after another.

I sighed to myself. Yes, he could have hit the other student when he threw the toy car, but I could feel his intent, and it wasn't to hurt the girl, who I also knew wouldn't be hurt. This time, though, I had to stop him.

If I had only him to worry about, I'd patiently wait for him to be done thrashing the cubby area and then set him on another track for the day, a fun task, before transitioning him to discussion mode—in which we would talk about and process his feelings—and then back to classroom mode. But I had others to think about. Like the kids who were now trying with everything they had to pay attention to their teacher while a peer of theirs not only touched their personal items, but treated those items with no care whatsoever.

"Okay, Joshua," I said in a relaxed voice. "How about we go throw things outside where it's safer."

He paused, lightly kicked a lunch pail onto the floor because he could, and exited the cubby.

I reached out my hand for him, but he sped past and bolted out the classroom door. Unattended children were a no-no in the kindergarten wing of the school, so I flashed a smile at Mrs. Elsworth, who mouthed *Thank you*, and ran after Joshua.

"No, this way," I called to him to get him to turn around and come closer to me. Redirecting to change their train of thought was a fabulous tool of mine.

Joshua paused, peered toward the door I motioned to, and as though I could see the thoughts in his head, walked back toward me.

Success.

He still refused to hold my hand.

"So"—I started our conversation before we even got to the playground—"how was your morning?"

A simple question that told me exactly how his day would unfold, how often I'd get called to Mrs. Elsworth's room.

He shrugged.

"That bad, huh?" I said with a laugh, trying to get him to relax enough to open up.

"No, not bad," he said, finally looking me in the eyes.

"Then what?" I asked as we walked slowly toward the playground and the metal bin of bouncy balls.

Rain misted onto us, but it didn't matter. We weren't going to play on the slides or the swings. We were headed to the basketball hoops under cover.

"I didn't have breakfast, but that's not bad," he stated matter-of-factly.

"It isn't?" I asked, urging him to go on.

He cocked his head and looked up in thought. "No," he said, deciding on his stance once we reached the court. "It's normal."

"But it makes you hungry, right? And that doesn't feel good," I said, grabbing a squishy red ball from the bin and tossing it to Joshua.

I realized, as I was saying the words, where my brain was leading us. Just because it's normal doesn't mean it's okay. And just because your brain says it's okay, if your body is saying something different, it's not really okay. Your body knows you far better than your brain.

He shrugged, but the wheels in his mind were spinning. I hoped if I brought it up enough—the idea of listening to his body—it would eventually stick.

That concept, listening to my body, rescued me from a mentally and emotionally abusive marriage. Being gaslit had become the norm in my home, and I'd lost the ability to listen to my own body, my own self. My ex's reasoning as to why he'd been right the whole time had permeated my mind and became my own inner voice. But my body, my body knew better.

This is how I connected to the naughty kids so well. The trauma in me saw the trauma in them.

Joshua tossed the ball to me, a softer smile on his lips, and the desire to play—in a healthy way—buzzing through his energy.

❖

Sarah

"So, this is where Oriana wants the yoga studio built," Faline said, leading Friday, Shawna, and me to the exact clearing I had watched the witch pour blood onto in the early hours of this morning.

So she'd been sanctifying the space. With blood. I shook my head. Sounded like an oxymoron to me. The only time a witch's blood sanctified anything was when it was spilled in death.

I froze.

I peered around with worry that the Wild Women in my presence saw my thoughts. Huldra weren't rusalki, the more psychic of the Wild Women, who I'd never met and was okay with that. Especially considering the horrid thoughts that sometimes surfaced from my subconscious Hunter brain.

"You okay?" Shawna asked. I focused on the here and now and saw the huldra's head tilted, her brows scrunched with concern.

I exhaled. "Yeah, just had a gross thought that had no business in my head."

Shawna gave a soft, knowing half smile and a nod.

"So," I started, to pay inner penance for thinking Oriana's blood was better spilled in death. *Why suffer a witch to live?* "How much do you know about this witch?"

Faline spun on her heel, bare feet on the moist pine needle-covered earth. "Oriana?"

I'd interrupted her planning the building of the yoga studio, but I couldn't get my mind to engage in the project until I cleared a few things up. It was a skill I picked up after watching the Hunter establishment I believed to be a permanent fixture of supernatural society—of my life—fall to the ground. If a Hunter lie crawled from its depths in my mind and got a foothold, I sought more information. It's how I learned about the Wild Women, how I met Faline and Shawna and their family. How I embraced my own abilities, as a woman who wasn't allowed to have them.

Humanizing those who are demonized does wonders toward putting hate to rest. It's the effort that counted, and I was trying.

"Yeah," I said. "Oriana. I know your clan wouldn't have sent you out here without a book of information gathered on this coven and the women in it."

Faline gave a laugh, and Shawna said, "She's not wrong."

Faline closed the gap between herself and an old evergreen. She gently rubbed the palm of her hand along its bark. Friday skipped over to sit facing the base of the tree and lean her forehead to its trunk.

"Oriana is the newest member to the Obsidian Falls coven," Faline started. "I'm told there's another witch in town, one not in the coven, but who'll eventually be the newest member, when it's time. Right now, it's Oriana's turn."

"Did the tree tell you that just now?" I asked, mystified.

Faline laughed. "No, my older sister has a thing for research."

Shawna half laughed.

"So, Oriana is the newest member?" I circled back and prodded for more.

"Yes, and she's new to the town too. Not just this property." Faline paused and closed her eyes, breathed in, and nodded. "She's already got other beings attracted to her property for solace."

I looked around and saw nothing.

"Anyway…" Faline exhaled and wiped her hands together. She moved from the old evergreen, but Friday kept her place at its base. "She's going through a divorce from an abusive ex, moved to a new town, got a new job, bought a new place. I can't imagine how she's navigating all this change so smoothly."

"Magic?" I asked, thinking of her in this place in the early morning hours, whispering prayers.

Shawna shook her head. "Magic with real witches isn't like in the movies. They kind of remind me of the rusalki. Their connection to nature gives them abilities, a little like us, but in different ways. More human ways?"

Since the fall of the Hunters and my introduction to Faline and her family via Marcus, every day brought a new revelation, a pulling back the curtain on all those things that go bump in the night. Witches, though, this was a first. And so far, I felt like a dog who'd just stepped off a rock into a deeper than expected body of water and was paddling for dear life.

It was new. It was different. And heck if some part of me didn't like it.

But I also knew there was a chance all this new could swallow me up, pull me under, and steal my breath.

No, that wasn't true. Yeah, this whole new life had definitely felt overwhelming at times, but not till I met Oriana had I ever felt breathless.

When Faline turned to peer back at the clearing with her hands on her hips, I requested more about Oriana.

"What kind of abuse?" I asked. As a female raised under the Hunter establishment and all the rules governing my mind and body that went along with it, I'd begun realizing that what I'd experienced had been emotional, mental, and spiritual abuse. Like an onion, the effects and lies had to be pulled back from my being, layer by layer, each exposing insidious lies meant to break my spirit, control me, relegate me to a life of servitude, and positioning me to be thankful for it.

Faline didn't respond. Her thoughts had gone back to yoga studio plans and that was that.

Shawna touched my arm and leaned in. "You should talk to Oriana, find out for yourself."

Honestly, the thought hadn't occurred to me.

"How?" I asked, feeling like a small child for the first time in...I had no idea how long.

Shawna smiled. Her dark brown eyes twinkled. "You've found a commonality with her. Go from there."

It was simple enough advice. Whether or not Oriana would want to talk to me after this morning's interaction was a whole other matter.

"Okay," Faline said, walking past Shawna and me, clearly on a mission. "Let's get started."

"Where's the plans?" I asked, following the huldra around the back of Oriana's home, to the truck and attached trailer. "I'll run and grab them."

Without turning around, Faline tapped the side of her head. "They're here."

She opened the side door to the big, white, enclosed trailer, grabbed the key from its place tucked into the inner left of the doorframe, and used it to unlock the padlock on the main door at the back of the trailer.

"Let's grab the beams and cement and get started on the base. It'd be awesome to have something in place when Oriana gets home from work."

I decided to use the deck beginnings as my conversation starter with Oriana, the way I would ease into my apology for this morning. I just needed to make sure we completed enough of the project to have something to talk about. I wasn't going to start by asking about her abuse, even if it was something we had in common.

Faline lowered and tilted her head at me, an amused expression that said *You with us?* on her face.

"I got it," I said, walking up to the back of the open trailer. Two-by-fours were stacked on each side, close to the wheel wells, with the heavier joist and metal L frames in the middle. I grabbed a few posts in each arm and took them to the clearing, as though I was merely holding piles of socks or some fabric. Hunter strength definitely had its perks.

I piled the wood to lean against a tree trunk, where it was safer from the rain and mud. "Let's get started."

Faline gave a nod and set a bucket of nails on top of the standing pile of boards I'd created.

Shawna winked as she handed me my black leather tool belt. I clicked the thing into place, hanging from my waist, caught on my hips. The handle of my hammer brushed my thigh and brought with it a single thought:

I hope Oriana comes home and sees me like this, swinging a hammer for her.

I caught my thoughts. No, I only wanted to have a real conversation with the witch to humanize her in my Hunter mind. To disprove the lies I'd been raised with, that had been ingrained in me.

That's it.

Nothing else.

No other reason to get to know Oriana. No other reason to spend time with her. God, I hoped I could disprove the lies about her.

I knew huldra weren't psychic, but the smile in Shawna's eyes when she watched me get to work made me wonder if she knew my thoughts.

Something told me she knew…even more than I did.

Chapter Nine

Oriana

Another hard day weighed on me. My shoulders hunched forward over the steering wheel with the invisible weight of failure as I slowly drove up the long, dark gravel driveway to my home.

No, I shouldn't call it failure. Although it felt like it. I'd thought I had been getting through to Joshua. I even started his day off on the right foot, following our talk on the playground while throwing the ball back and forth. But after lunch, he had started his antics again, and before they could call me, he actually did hit a classmate by throwing a block. His dad had been called, and he was sent home for the rest of the day.

Another day of school that little boy would miss because the adults in his life failed him. Tonight, I counted myself among them.

I parked behind the truck and trailer and trudged up to my porch and front door, stomping the earth from my shoes on each step. I really needed to put down some gravel or something because I would go through shoes too quickly for my budget if I caked mud on them each time I came home or left.

Hammers banged back in the clearing behind my house, the bang resonating through the woods, bouncing off the evergreens.

I moaned inwardly. I really didn't feel like entertaining anyone. Tonight, I just wanted to throw sweats on and binge watch *Hoarders*. It was my go-to on mental health days—to watch other forms of mental health issues, the kind that are obvious, the kind people wear on their sleeves, the manifestation of some undealt-with trauma.

Shows like *Hoarders* made me feel better. Especially on days like today, when I was too mentally and emotionally exhausted to fight the nagging voice in my head suggesting I made this all up and left my marriage and my life for no good reason. When I couldn't be my own pick-me-up, shows like this did it for me. Reminded me that yes, mental health issues exist, and yes, I'm not alone in the world, I'm not the only person having to deal with the effects of trauma.

At least I was dealing with my issues, a little further in the healing process. It gave me hope to see people stand up against their damaging cycles and get help to change the way they operated.

Still, watching little Joshua walk out of the office with a very angry dad who'd had to leave work to get his naughty kid made me feel like a failure.

I'd failed this innocent kid who'd had so many other adults—who should have known better—fail him.

Back when I was with my ex-husband, when I had come home beaten down from failing a child, he had reminded me that the world was an awful place, and not to care so much about one person who would end up in jail eventually anyway. At the time, I had the bad habit of listening and believing him, even if only temporarily until logic reminded me of truth.

Now I tried to see Steven for who he was, whenever his words pierced my thoughts and took over my mind. His beliefs about the world and his condemnation of an innocent and hurting child he had never met were nothing more than him not giving a shit about anyone but himself. Saying the world is a crappy place, so don't try, is his way of saying nothing is worth his effort but him.

Narcissists have a twisted way of viewing the world. A hopeless way, really.

I removed my shoes, their soles still caked with mud despite my stomping, and passed the couch and remote. Later. I'd rest and relax with some depressing, yet hopeful reality TV later. Right now, I had a little girl with gifts beyond my comprehension to hang with, and Wild Women building my future—a yoga studio to teach my passion for healing—to cook a meal for.

I hung my head out the back door mudroom and called into the fading light. I couldn't see the Wild Women, but I heard them working, and I knew they had sensitive hearing. So I called out, "Friday! Want to help me cook dinner?"

The hammering paused, and Friday burst through the woods to my back porch. She tramped up the porch steps, a huge grin from ear to ear. The moment her bare foot touched the first step, the hammering resumed.

"You like to cook?" I asked.

She gave a big nod.

"Perfect," I said, "because we are going to make sage chicken and use sage from my own plant." I led her inside and grabbed a hand towel from the kitchen drawer. I set her on the counter to clean and dry her feet. "I've got a happy sage bush to gather the sage from. Have you ever gathered natural food for a meal?"

She shook her head.

"Okay, well, the first thing you need to know when gathering living food is to ask their permission."

Any human child would ask how I'd go about getting permission from a plant, but Friday seemed to know exactly what I was referring to. She gave a nod.

"They don't like when you steal from them," she added.

"No one wants to share their creation with the world before they've fully completed it," I said. "Including plants. They have a process, and when we take from them without their permission, it interrupts that process, weakens them."

"They like me, though," the five-year-old said, and I couldn't help but laugh in response.

"Yes, they do," I said around a snicker. "But back to the plants and harvesting their creations—as long as you only pluck their creation, you're not hurting them. It's when you uproot them, when you overpick and pick too early, that you run the chance of damaging or killing them." I paused in thought. I didn't normally talk like this with little ones, but Friday was special. No denying it. "There are ways to work in harmony with all living beings on this planet. And I think…" The realization occurred to me as I spoke. "And I think that's what I'm supposed to teach you. How to work in harmony."

It made no sense. The child was huldra and xana—her maternal grandmother tree woman, and her paternal grandmother water woman.

She was, just by being herself, the epitome of connection with nature. Harmony was probably a no-brainer for her, something she didn't need to think about because it came so naturally.

But I had to go with my intuition.

"I think I'm supposed to teach you about energy," I said to her as though I was informing a teenager or even an adult.

Her little nose scrunched as she considered this fact. "What is energy?" she asked.

I smiled. Yup, that was it.

I took her off the counter and pulled the chicken breasts from the refrigerator. "Energy is everything, and everything is energy," I started. I unwrapped the chicken and set the slimy meat on a plate.

"Chicken is energy?" Friday asked.

I laughed inwardly. Of course the child wouldn't ask this question of plants. She knew their energy, she felt it. But a piece of meat...

I made a mental note not to try to teach her about the energy of plants—she already felt their essence, even if she didn't technically know what they were or why, even if she hadn't uncovered their truths yet.

Or maybe I shouldn't be teaching her energy at all. What if I was wrong and only confusing her?

An unnerving blanket of self-doubt draped itself over my shoulders enough to cause my chest to roll forward and my pelvis to tuck in.

Friday noticed because she cocked her head for a short moment and then switched her focus to pulling a table chair over to the counter where I leaned, my hair nearly brushing the raw chicken. I just had to center myself again.

Sometimes the self-doubt had a debilitating physical impact. If I could just breathe and recite a truth shown to me by the spirits...

Except the truth was nowhere to be found in my mind. Only the reminder that a child was hurt today and Joshua had to miss school as a result, which was proof I didn't know what I was doing when it came to kids.

My cell phone buzzed on the table ten feet away, in the dining area adjoining the kitchen.

Happy for the distraction, I ripped a section of paper towel from its roll and used it as a barrier between my chicken slime hands and the phone. No name popped up on the screen, just numbers indicating the call came from my old hometown.

I answered the call. "Hi!" I almost sounded cheery.

The response, though, was very much not cheery.

"Oriana," my ex-husband said, his voice tender and thoughtful. "Are you ready to discuss that financial thing?"

I slumped against the wooden tabletop.

His gestures of empathy were only sleights of hand, him preparing to unsheathe the knife.

"I told you, Steven," I started, giving him the same answer to the same question he repeatedly forgot he had asked, "there is nothing to discuss. We had a shared bank account at the time. My paycheck was automatically being deposited into our joint account. Our joint account was where the money came from to pay off that credit card statement."

I couldn't say for a fact he forgot. But from what the spirits have shown me, people with his disorder, narcissistic personality disorder, operate their daily lives off a script they live by, their own production or play. Certain types of trauma, they tell me, impact certain parts of the brain, change particular ways of thinking and being. In the way a cold is caused by a certain virus and gives the sick person particular symptoms, each different type of trauma hits a particular part of the brain and causes certain symptoms.

Kids who grow up with emotionally neglectful parents, who are often narcissistic themselves, can create an alternate reality for themselves, one in which they are important and loved. One in which they are the center—the main character. That world is much more livable and they tend to stay there the rest of their days. To maintain that world, they require all those around them, the participants in their play, to comply with the script. If they don't, they are either cast out of the play, discarded, or given a new role as the villain. Once you're in the villain role, you live there the rest of your days.

I should know. I'm the villain in Steven's play.

I try to remind myself of this, try to reassure myself that the triggers swirling inside, those dark and heavy feelings of shame and guilt, are not my own but the result of years of his placing the blame of his unhappiness onto me. Because the main character can't be the cause.

His words pick away at my resolve, as though picking at a scab he won't let heal. "It's just, you said you'd pay me back."

See, this is a formulated attack, I told myself. *He started with thoughtful. He's now at guilting, and next he'll start in on blame-throwing.* It's like flamethrowing in that it happens suddenly, causes great pain, and leaves a lifetime of scars. Only, unlike actual flames, his words cast scars on me that only I can see.

"I did," I try to say calmly and without an ounce of emotion. I can't let him see me have an emotional reaction. In the end, that's what he's aiming for. Positive or negative, it doesn't matter to him either way. The goal is to know he's important enough to hit a nerve. "But you are leaving out the part where I later came to my senses and explained logic to you."

Shit. I let a drop of irritation seep through that last part.

My whole body tensed in preparation.

"You got a hotel room, Oriana. A fucking hotel room." He spat the words as though I was the dirtiest slut he'd ever encountered. "On our joint credit card. While we were married." He said *married* as though he'd spent our relationship respecting and honoring the institution. He hadn't. Not by a long shot.

I should have shaken my head at his nonsense and continued my evening as though someone of no consequence, who didn't know me, had said something totally inaccurate about me. I should have. But I didn't. I couldn't.

My heart raced and my hands shook. Coldness swept through my limbs and climbed into my core, freezing me from the inside out until my whole body vibrated.

"You," I stuttered into the phone. Tears filled my eyes. The panic attack was coming, and I was powerless to stop it. I hated being powerless.

Yes, I'd gotten a hotel room, to get away from him—a sweet reprieve—for one night. I'd already told him I wanted a divorce. He'd agreed. He'd been wanting one for years, anyhow. He had brought it up each time I refused to bend to his will. So we had separated and pursued divorce. It was what we both wanted.

Until I performed an unbinding spell the full moon night I removed my wedding band. After that, he changed his mind and wanted me back. I refused. Nearly each time we were home at the same time, he followed me around the house, taking turns berating me and declaring his love for me, as though he held two flags, one green and one red, and whichever he chose to hold up mattered little to him. What he wanted was a reaction, the exact thing I refused to give him, which tended to leave me with more red flags than green.

The night I had gotten a hotel room had been the night I'd had too much of waiting for him to move out, as he'd promised. That's the night I sat on the queen bed, stared for hours at a painting of a boat, and decided to move out of our house and our town, for good. Decided I had been drowning for far too long. It was time to offer myself a flotation device.

And yet he had told all our friends and family that I'd cheated on him that night I'd gone to a hotel.

The day I got that phone call from a cousin, asking why I had done such a thing to my husband...

My world had collapsed.

The shame and guilt I'd been pressured to carry with no knowledge of it being placed on my back came barreling back down onto me, threatening to crush me.

I couldn't breathe under the weight. I had to get out.

Steven yelled my name from the other end of the call, as though I was behaving like an insolent child.

He had me where he wanted, diving into an emotional tailspin.

I tried to sputter out a response, but my blank mind produced nothing more than fear-riddled fragments of thought. The cell phone slipped from my fingers, and I slid to the floor, my knees too weak and shaky to carry my own weight and that which had been set upon me.

At the periphery of my mind, Friday jumped from the chair and bolted from the kitchen, out the back door, screaming for her mother, for help.

Tears poured from my face and sobs racked my body at the touch of hands picking me up carefully and sturdily, and cradling me. She squeezed me against her chest and tucked her face over mine as she carried me from the kitchen and down the back porch steps. I wasn't wearing shoes, and the outside chill caused me to shake harder.

So she held me tighter.

"It'll be okay," she breathed out in a whisper. "I'm taking you to your tree."

I cried again, only in thanksgiving and relief this time. I didn't have a tree guide yet, but I figured any tree could help ground me at this point.

Night air greeted us, and I breathed it in, trying to imagine the air cleansing my hurt, healing my heart and mind. I was too fragmented to envision negativity away and gave up, slouching my cheek against the top of her chest. She smelled like pine and flowers, the most comforting scent ever.

"I'm broken," I cried to Sarah. "He broke me."

"No," she assured me. "You're hurting. Hurting is temporary. Broken isn't." Seconds later, she said, "We're here. I'm going to set you down."

I wanted to respond but couldn't bring myself to speak or move. As though someone had taken a syringe and drained me of my last ounce of energy, I lay in her arms, too lethargic to lift my head.

Only then did I realize she'd calmed me enough to be tired, to no longer shake and convulse.

She gently placed me facing the tree, within arm's length, and backed away. The wet ground seeped through my pants, and my bare heels sank into the soft pine-needle-covered dirt. I reached for the tree and brushed my fingers across the bark. With as much energy as I could muster, I scooted my butt forward until I could wrap my arms around the evergreen and lean my forehead to its trunk.

A light tree energy greeted me, but it felt nothing like what I needed. To receive energy from plants, you have to meet them halfway. Or least a quarter of the way. I had nearly nothing to give. I leaned my head enough to motion to Sarah.

She ran over and crouched behind me. "What is it?" she asked, concern filling her voice.

"I can't do it on my own," I whispered, embarrassed at my complete vulnerability in front of a stranger, a Wild Woman no less.

"What do you need me to do?" she asked, ready and willing to do whatever it took. I didn't need to turn and look at her eyes to know. I could feel it radiating off her.

My shoulders eased down a centimeter or so, and I found myself able to take a breath. "I need you to sit like I am, but around me, while I'm around the tree."

It was a lot to ask a stranger, but desperate times…

And anyway, she knew what I asked of her. She was a Wild Woman. They were acquainted with the energy transference of nature.

She crawled down to me and wrapped her arms around mine, her legs outside mine, as though she covered me like a shield at my back, facing the outside world, protecting me, allowing me space to heal. I silently thanked her and began pulling energy through her to me.

Like sturdy threads, energy eased from Sarah and into me. Inside of my being, I balled the threads of energy and pushed them into the tree to create an energetic connection wherever the bark and I touched. Mere seconds ticked by before the tree responded with bursts of plant energy, which reminded me of roots, anchoring me to the earth.

Through this process Sarah's essence, bits of her being, of who she was, became apparent to me, introduced themselves to my energy. I thanked her again silently and continued pulling energy from her, envisioning it pass through me and enter the tree. I envisioned the tree absorbing it into its roots, dispersing it among its kind, and then in return, pushing plant energy into me, reaching and stopping in Sarah's back.

She sighed and loosened her body, leaning forward into me. This time, I could handle the weight. Thanks to her.

My heart slowed with each pulse of energy. My brain cleared. My muscles let go. My jaw unclenched. I allowed my lungs to fill and empty. Fill and empty.

I opened my eyes and turned my head enough to see Sarah's head leaning just slightly on my right shoulder. Her eyes fluttered closed with the plant energy. I'd never seen her brows so unserious looking. Her jaw slackened. Her lips parted.

As though she felt my thought, saw the sudden image in my mind of me kissing her, of feeling her breath on my mouth, her eyes opened softly. We focused on one another. I watched her soft gaze bounce to my lips and then back to my stare. She gave the tiniest of nods, and maybe it was the shared plant energy flowing through us, but everything in me knew what she was saying yes to.

I pressed my lips to hers. And I kissed her.

I kissed a Wild Woman. And I more than liked it…

I fucking loved it.

CHAPTER TEN

Sarah

Once, when I was little, I woke from the most serene dream. It had taken place in the woods, which wasn't a huge deal seeing as we Hunters' daughters were familiar with nature in the way someone highly allergic to flowers is aware of the flora in their area.

Basically, we weren't taken to the woods to hunt animals and play war games like the boys I'd grown up with, but we were given limited access to the sinister secrets of nature, how many unique and terrifying ways a helpless little girl can die by the hand of Mother Nature.

As a girl, that alone, the deadliness of nature, is what drew me to it. What had been meant to deter me only spurred a secret obsession. Each time I stepped into the woods—which was less often once I'd reached a marriageable age—a sense of aliveness filled me. They weren't just trees I gazed up at in awe. They were beings capable of the worst torture, able to be manipulated by huldra. Whenever an eagle flew overhead or a hawk, I didn't only see a great bird. I saw the cousins to the Harpies who could swoop down without notice and slice me open with one talon.

The woods belonged to the Wild Women—hell, nature was the Wild Woman's playground and sanctuary and home. She was nature and nature was her. One could not exist without the other.

So when the sensation of what I can only explain as the cleanest, warmest, most comforting water seeped into my being without a drop of liquid...I melted. It was as though an ache I'd held buried inside made itself known, and a soothing liquid-free water acted as balm to reach in and pull out my desire to know more, to explore this thing called nature. Had this been what Oriana meant when she'd asked if she could pull energy through me?

Had I just experienced her witch energy?

I lay on the couch in Oriana's dark living room. Her forced-air heat clicked on and off, announcing its stop and start with bangs and clangs behind the wall nearest my head. That wasn't what was keeping me up, though, while the rest of the house slept. A more worrying question scratched at the edges of my thoughts, and I pushed it back. I much preferred reliving the way Oriana touched me with those magical hands, the way she seemed to see into me, accepted me.

But if she saw into me, then did she see my Hunter? Growing up, it was always the boys who were talked to about their inner Hunter as a separate and equal part of who they were. Girls were never included in this, but tonight I felt my Hunter deep within, opening her sleepy eyes.

Had the witch meant to bring this monster out? Had nature intended to do it? Was that the cost of connecting with nature, to be splayed open and have light shined into the darkest and most hidden sides of yourself? I pondered the thought a while, only breaking long enough to be jarred by the heater turning on and off.

I should have felt fear or at least tension. My body knew that was supposed to happen, my mind continually reminded me of it. But Oriana's energy still flowed through me.

I sat up on the couch. Clock hands ticked in the darkness. That was what woke up my Hunter, wasn't it?

My heart sped, but not toward any impulse or worry. It sped with knowing. And was that excitement? I smiled to myself. The presence of Wild Women had never physically affected me.

Well, I mean, I was attracted to women, so clearly there was a reaction around Wild Women, but never from my inner Hunter. Now, a light thrum of electricity vibrated from inside, almost a stretching and flexing. My Hunter. She felt Wild Women in the house.

I knew Faline and Shawna posed absolutely no threat, but my Hunter seemed to wonder about them from a place of foggy confusion. This should have scared me, the disorientation and sudden desire to question my friends who slept down the hall from me, but it didn't.

Something I hadn't realized was missing finally returned. A part of me I never felt belonged suddenly clicked into place and made me feel whole for the first time in my life.

Talk about an aha moment.

Shame trickled through me, following close behind my excitement and nearly catching up to engulf whatever positive emotions blossomed within. The more I concentrated on my Hunter, the more I felt her—the way she paced inside, clearly trapped in a home with Wild Women and unsure how to proceed.

I found my gaze focusing on the hallway. Wild Women slept behind one of those doors. Dangerous Wild Women.

I silently slapped my hand over my mouth and shook my head. No, I couldn't think that way about my family, about the women who had supported me and given me their shoulders to cry on. But my Hunter had no ears for that sort of love and loyalty.

I peered at the darkened screen on my cell phone and thought to shoot Marcus a text, something along the lines of *Oh crap, help.* I reached for the device and pulled back suddenly, as though an unseen force smacked my hand away.

What could Marcus say to help? What could he do, not being allowed on witch property?

Nothing. He could do nothing.

Panic set in.

What if Oriana hadn't been able to tell I was a Hunter because my Hunter had stayed hidden, even from me? And now she wasn't hidden. Now she stretched and yawned and wiped the sleep from her eyes. What would she see when she fully awakened? What would she insist upon? What would she do?

"Sarah," a voice whispered, as quiet and powerful as the wind.

I stood at the ready to defend myself. But I said nothing. Confusion and fear and anger taunted me from the edges of my mind, none showing themselves enough for me to bat them away with some logical explanation.

"Sarah," the voice said again, this time at the end of the hallway leading to Faline's room, where she slept with Shawna and Friday.

I rushed to the Wild Women's door to press my ear to the faux wood.

Nothing.

"Sarah," the voice repeated, as though the mouth speaking my name did so from an inch in front of my face. Fear played with my senses and rattled in my legs, demanding I run. This time, though, I didn't react. I listened.

Definitely female.

And definitely taunting me. But why?

I waited for her to call my name again, sing it in a teasing game of catch me if you can. I filed through my memories of different types of Wild Women and which were able to throw their voices or play games with the mind and ears. A list came to mind, but the only Wild Women I knew of that were capable were friends of mine or friends of Faline's. They wouldn't taunt me, or lurk around this temporary territory of Faline's without a courteous heads-up.

"I asked you to stop." The words were not mine. They came from a witch on the other side of the house, Oriana.

Before I realized or even thought to move, I stood outside her door, listening for signs of a struggle, or basically any reason to burst through her bedroom door. Silence.

And then, sobbing.

CHAPTER ELEVEN

Sarah

My hands clenched as I stood outside Oriana's bedroom door, as I shifted my weight from one foot to the other and back. I didn't know what to do. Go in and announce that I'd heard her crying...and then what?

No. I shoved my hands in my pajama pant pockets and paced a three-step line, back and forth, back and forth, in front of her door, which faced the dining area and kitchen. Her bedroom wall separated her from the couch I had been sleeping on. I could just go back and rest and listen for her on my side of the wall.

Except nothing in me allowed me to leave this spot. I had to stand outside her door like a guard. The more I got to know Oriana, the more I wanted to make sure she was happy, she was safe, she was comfortable.

I had felt something similar for my found family, my Wild Women friends, but not to this extent.

I sensed no other physical being in the home, and yet everything in me knew Oriana was in real danger and needed me *now*. No. No. She was alone, in her room, maybe voice texting or something. Yeah. That was it.

Except as much as my mind insisted on logic and reality, my heart and everything else in me refused to get on board. Oriana was upset, and I could feel it in my bones. She didn't deserve this. She deserved happiness and joy and kisses and hugs...and me.

No. What?

My thoughts tripped over themselves for a quick second before

Oriana's quiet sobs brought my focus back where it belonged. To the woman behind the door.

But where had this sense of protection come from? It doubled by the minute now, and yet I hadn't known her more than a day or two.

At least I had enough sanity left to make a mental note to text Marcus in the morning—being a female Hunter had very quickly become more than I knew how to handle. Especially since getting off the ironically named *vitamins*.

"You promised, though, Steven. You promised." Oriana's defeated voice shook me.

I couldn't stop myself. And frankly, I didn't want to. Didn't she deserve someone to give a crap? Didn't she deserve me to give a crap? Didn't she deserve me?

In one silent jerk, I whipped open the door, imagining I would find some masked man in Oriana's bedroom, pushing himself on her. Instead, I found her propped in the center of her bed, in the dark, hunched over a cell phone, its light illuminating her face, a sheen of tears covering her cheeks. She barely looked up, as though she only had enough energy to move her neck slightly. Her blank yet pain-stricken eyes found mine and pleaded silently for respite.

I glared at the phone. In the place of the name of whoever she spoke with on-screen, I read *Do Not Answer*.

Not a good sign. More like a sign that read *Danger, problems ahead*.

A problem I intended to fix.

I leaned toward her slowly, and as my hand neared her phone, she only watched. We both knew my next move was for the better.

In one quick easy tap, I did what it appeared she couldn't. I hung up on whichever bastard thought they could talk to Oriana like that. She still held the phone tightly when I slipped my hand over hers and waited for her to loosen her grip, for her to let it fall into my palm. If he called again, I didn't want her having to know. I wanted to save her the stress. If she let me.

Keeping my fingers in place under hers, and trying not to get caught up in the way hers felt so natural over mine, the way her skin belonged next to mine, I lowered my body to the bed and sat in front of her. The two of us faced one another on her white comforter, staring into eyes and hands clasped, and hovered around a phone. She only stared and I only waited.

Until a thought occurred to me. "Are you deciding whether or not to let me?" It was as though I could feel her desire to allow me to help her, but also her fear, her hesitance.

Knowing—or was it the shock of being seen?—flashed in her eyes, and she released the phone into my hand. In an instant I tucked it behind me and slid it into the back pocket of my flannel pajama pants. I considered getting this asshat's phone number from her phone and possibly seeing why he thought it was okay to make someone like Oriana, someone caring and selfless and so beautiful, cry. Only a monster would think that's all right. And didn't Hunters handle monsters?

But I needed to keep focus on Oriana. The bastard didn't deserve preferential treatment. She did.

"Will you tell me what happened?" I asked as gently as I could, the tenderness forced to squeeze out and around the angry Hunter inside set on tracking down Oriana's monster.

I waited through the quiet moments in the dark room. For the first time, I looked around. Even if I had the abilities of a Hunter male, I wouldn't be able to see in the dark. But my eyes had adjusted enough for me to make out a painting of the moon phases above her bedroom window, and a Pride flag draped along her wall like a tapestry.

Finally, she spoke in a hushed tone as though we'd be heard. I had no doubt if a Wild Woman was up, we *were* being heard. Oriana may have known that too, but something about her tone spoke more of fear than privacy.

"I know what he's doing," she whispered. "My brain knows." She shook her head. "My fucking heart, though. Fuck my heart." That last part had an edge to it I didn't much care for—dark and hurting and tougher than she looked comfortable being.

"He's not worth ignoring your heart for," I found myself saying.

"He's not worth following my heart, either," she muttered sarcastically.

I thought back to those times all I wanted was for someone to crack open my heart and peek inside, see the pain and offer to hold it for me, offer to help carry the load and sort through the crap pile of emotions and confusion alongside me. I considered my years of longing for a trust so secure, a love so genuine, that they would know when to draw near, when to hold my aching heart and give me a respite.

I couldn't be sure where all my considering left me, but I did know one thing in that moment: Oriana's heart was a frontier, vast and deep, that beckoned my exploration.

"What does your head know about him? About all of this?" I asked.

She gave a nod and took a cleansing breath. Clearly it was easier for her to talk about what she knew than what she felt. "Steven has NPD."

I used her pause to ask, "What's that stand for?" Mental health wasn't exactly a priority in the Hunter community. Feelings lied and therapists were quacks, said the men with raging control issues and the women with Stockholm syndrome. *That* one I did know. The huldra had mentioned it a time or two to describe the dynamic between my mother and father.

She didn't look away from the comforter. "It stands for narcissistic personality disorder."

"So he's incredibly self-centered?" I asked. "That would make sense for the middle of the night phone call."

She smirked, but not for any kind of delight. "I wish." She shook her head. "Actually, I don't wish because then I'd probably still be with him, and I never want that again."

God, I wanted to ask her what that meant, wanted to know more about what she looks for in a mate, but that was my own selfishness wondering. I stuffed those questions down and kept the topic on her, helping her unpack twisted feelings and thoughts.

"If he was just selfish, he'd just be a narcissist or have narcissistic tendencies," she continued. "But no, he fits the requirements for an NPD diagnosis. He literally can't self-actualize. Others may assume he can with what he says and because it's normal human behavior to be able to, to some degree. But he doesn't even comprehend what it truly is. Anything he says with depth or empathy is only regurgitated sayings he's heard from others. He figures it's what people want to hear."

She quieted again, as though she was retreating into her thoughts, so I pulled her out to continue with one word. "Okay?"

She exhaled. "He has delusions of grandeur, which is another big indicator. In his head, he deserves the best of the best, and not because he's earned it in any way, just because he's him."

"Did he consider you the best of the best?" I asked, curious.

Tears streamed down her face at my question.

Regret washed over me. I shouldn't have asked that. "I'm sorry," I said.

She placed a hand on my knee and held it there while still peering at the ground. "No, it's okay. He did consider me worthy at first. It's what they do. It's called love-bombing. The best way I've heard people with NPD explained is that to them, the world is a play they wrote with characters they cast. If they find a person they believe can fit the part, they're excited to basically find another piece of their puzzle, what'll make them happy, someone who fits into their narration."

She pulled her hand back, and her voice changed only slightly, but enough for my Hunter to pick up on. "But none of their characters are people to them, so when they start to see you won't fit perfectly into their story, they begin to devalue you and end up discarding you. For some it's a year-after-year cycle of love-bombing, devaluing, and discarding."

"Was it like that for you?" I asked, my attention fully on her, her hurt, her recollection of the past, her heart.

"For a little while, yeah," she answered. "But my work with special-needs kids as a paraeducator started showing me different types of behavioral issues. Especially with the naughty kids' parents. A big one for me was the lack of empathy. When I brought this up to Steven, as a possible reason we were having issues, he raged. And when that didn't work to keep my empathy questions at bay, he switched tactics and threatened to leave me if I didn't drop it, if I didn't make our home life good again for him. He even went so far as to call me broken and suggest I see a therapist about that."

"Wow," was all I could say. Holy crap. I'd been around some wild stuff in the Hunter community—controlling men, manipulating leaders. But none lacked empathy, that I knew of, even if they'd only had it for their fellow brothers. At least they had it.

"So I went to see a therapist," she continued.

I turned to her, shocked. In response she met my gaze. "Why would you do that? Clearly he's the broken one."

Her swollen eyes softened, and the hint of a smile lifted her lips ever so slightly. "Remember the love-bombing I told you about?"

I gave a quick nod.

"That's how they hook you," she said. "They convince you of their undying love and devotion and that you two are so alike and have so much in common. In reality they are mirroring you so you'll trust them, but who would think that when it's happening? It feels so good. So real. So when they devalue you—or, in my case, tell you you're broken—you trust that this is coming from a place of love and wanting to help."

"Even when you already knew he didn't have empathy?" I asked.

"Yeah, at that point I had a couple of the pieces but hadn't put them together to know what I was dealing with. I just knew I was breaking inside and felt broken and needed help."

I put my hand on her thigh, and she placed hers over mine, as if to welcome the touch and thank me. My stomach stirred with the excitement of feeling her, and I inwardly told it to shut the hell up. Not the time for that.

"After seeing the therapist weekly for a few months, she pointed out the pattern she'd seen during our time together," Oriana continued. "He blamed me and others for all his unhappiness. When I didn't comply with what he said he needed, he'd throw an adult fit. When I did comply, he'd be fine and happy again until something else happened in his perfectly crafted life to upset him again, and then he'd start all over again, blaming me and insisting I make things right."

"What did your therapist say you should do at the time?" I asked.

Oriana lifted her hand from mine just long enough to wipe her eyes. She set it back down, and immediately I felt better, having her skin touch mine.

She laughed a short laugh. "She told me to go online, look up personality disorders, and read through all of them. She wanted me to come back the following week and tell her which disorders I thought he fit, and we'd discuss."

"And he fit the NPD one?"

She smiled this time, a real smile, though it didn't reach her eyes and it didn't last long. "Yeah. His lack of empathy is what hit it home for me."

She turned toward me on the bed, her legs still folded into one another like a pretzel. "They've done brain scans of people with NPD and seen that the empathy portion of their brain isn't lit up like most people's. Isn't that extraordinary?"

Now that Oriana's mood seemed to shift, I brought up the original issue of the evening, what she'd said she needed help with, without saying she needed help. "So if your head knows all of that, that it's him, that he can't love and won't love, that he can't care about anyone other than himself because to him, others aren't real people with thoughts and feelings, then what is your heart having a hard time with?"

She sighed and dropped her head. I turned my hand over so that my palm faced hers, and I wove my fingers into hers, out of worry she'd pull away and emotionally retreat.

"My heart wants to take half the blame. I still care for him, and I see he's hurting, and I want to help by making it better," she answered.

"Even though you know nothing you can do will make it better."

"Yeah," she said on a sigh.

"What about you?" I asked.

"What about me?" she responded.

"You're hurting. How do you make yourself feel better?"

I took her silence to mean I should elaborate. Or maybe the lack of words between us made me uncomfortable. Either way, I kept talking. "If you know there's nothing you can do to make him feel better, truly feel better not just satiate him in the moment, then you also know the only person you can make feel better is yourself."

She paused as though she'd never considered herself in that way before. And maybe she hadn't. I knew I rarely considered myself as important, as deserving of compassion and love. Not in the way I considered others to be.

"Time will make me feel better, I guess," she said. "Time away from him. No contact. My head knows I'm not a person to him," she added, "and that I should just let him drown in his own pool of mistakes. But my heart, my heart can't let him."

"Is it your heart or your hurt that can't let him drown?" I asked before weighing whether or not my question was appropriate, something I seemed to do often with this witch.

Her shoulders slumped more. "See now, that's opening up a whole can of worms I'm not sure I'm ready to handle."

I nodded because that's all I could do, and because I understood.

If she recognized her hurt drove her actions, then she'd have to dig into that hurt, learn about it, where it came from, why it was there, to remove it. Oh, I knew the truths of the matter all too well.

I wondered how closely she felt her life represented the rectangular moon phases painting on her wall.

Oriana yawned and didn't hide it with her hand. I felt foolish for noticing and even more so for thinking it was cute that she didn't feel the need to be polite in front of me.

She needed rest. Did witches need sleep like humans? I wasn't sure, but I also wasn't about to leave her alone. I told myself she needed someone, she needed me, to comfort her. But in reality, I wanted to be who she needed to comfort her, and I figured I'd deal with the ramifications later.

"Here," I said, standing to smooth out her comforter. I pulled her phone from my back pocket to show her what I was doing. "I'm going to block his number on your phone, is that okay?"

She nodded with another open-mouthed yawn and crawled to her pillow as though she accepted my offer of comfort. I hoped that's what she was doing, anyway.

I pulled up recent calls, looked for the *do not answer* account, and blocked all texts and calls. By the time I finished, Oriana had buried herself in blankets—lying on her side away from me, facing her nightstand—and rested her head on her pillow. When I reached over her shoulders to place the phone on her nightstand, she grabbed my forearm and wrapped it around her right biceps.

She wanted me to spoon her.

She wanted me to be the big spoon.

Me.

I'd never spooned anyone, least of all a gorgeous woman.

But here she was, not letting go of my arm. And Lord, I hoped she never would.

I strategically lowered my body behind hers, still lending my arm to her embrace. How would it feel to have my whole body in her arms? Probably like heaven because just having my arm laid over her ribs and waist made my brain go numb and my heart beat into overdrive.

I lay behind her but made sure not to actually touch her back to my front. I didn't want to look pervy, especially while she needed emotional support. But apparently, she was not concerned because once I stilled into place, she shifted and scooted, booty first, right into me.

I froze.

Until I realized she probably felt me stiffen. She didn't need to be thinking about my comfort in a moment like this. I told my now nonstop-chatting brain to shut the hell up, and within seconds my muscles eased. As though I'd been cuddling with her for the last year, I melted into her. Where she stopped and I started, I didn't want to know. I couldn't think of anything feeling this right, this perfect.

I forced my smile off my face, didn't want to look like a fool, but my heart smiled for the first time ever. This woman, her bed, her scent—patchouli and lavender—felt like home. More than home, more than what I'd always known home to feel like. Oriana felt like magic. And I hoped she'd let me stay under her spell. I wished she didn't hate Hunters. But mostly, I hoped when she found out what I really was, she wouldn't hate me for it.

CHAPTER TWELVE

Oriana

Sarah's comfort was like someone handing me a tall glass of ice water after I'd worked in the yard on a hot summer afternoon. Like a foot soak and massage after a day of marching in a protest. In her arms, I could rest.

Sarah was like nothing I'd ever felt before. I wished I could extend my energy into hers and feel her being, know her emotions in this moment, but I had already tried and…nothing.

It wasn't her fault, it was mine. And really no one's *fault*. To make that happen, I needed a certain energetic key that I just couldn't muster at the moment, a vibration higher than my current state. Every time Steven did this, it fucked with my head and my energy.

He was the reason I got into yoga, into therapy, into self-healing. He was unhappy because of me, so I went to a therapist to learn what was wrong with me that I couldn't even make the love of my life happy. Turns out he wasn't the love of my life. It was all a sham. But hey, I got some amazing coping skills out of it.

Sarah inhaled deeply, and I hoped she was smelling me. Not because I'm weird, but because it meant she liked me. Because I liked her. How she looked, how quiet and reserved she was, the way she appeared to be thinking and feeling nothing but on the inside lived a beautiful storm of wonder and emotions. At least that's what I felt when I pushed my energy through her earlier, in the woods.

I never would have guessed the depth to her soul before that.

And now tonight, with the way she comforted me? I wanted to know everything about her. Why did she hold back so much? What did she really think about my place, my yoga studio plans?

What did she think about me?

Why did it matter? Why should it matter? I was in no place to be with anyone, to give a person love and care when I was only just learning what those things were and trying desperately to apply them to myself.

Did I even have enough love for myself to extend some to another? I wasn't so sure. I made a mental note to discuss this question with my coven sisters next moon and tucked the query away for that time.

Now was not the moment to be thinking of existential things, not when a beautiful woman, inside and out, lay behind me, holding me in her arms. In this moment, in this room, in this bed, the world was right and everything made sense.

I brought the back of her hand to my cheek and nuzzled it, unable to get close enough to her. I'd thought the closeness would sweetly lull me to sleep, but something else stirred deep in my belly and crawled south.

I hadn't meant to, but I kissed the back of her hand. And then her wrist.

In response, I felt a soft kiss on the back of my head.

My stomach fluttered and my senses begged for more of Sarah, more of her skin, more of her scent, her feel, the sound of her breath.

I rolled over and our eyes met. "What's your sign?" I asked out of nowhere.

She cocked her head. "I don't want to tell you. You'll judge me."

I laughed. "Judge you for something you can't help? Okay, I'll go first then."

I made a show of revealing my embarrassing nature by covering my eyes when I said it. "I'm an Aries."

I pulled my hand away to gauge her expression.

"Do you know what Aries is?" I asked, because her response told me she didn't.

"Yeah, fiery and impulsive," Sarah said with a short laugh.

"Okay, then," I said. "I shared mine, now you share yours."

A different meaning to my statement flashed in her eyes for a split second before she settled a more friendly gaze on me. "People don't hate Aries like they hate Geminis."

"*You* are a Gemini?" I asked, surprised.

Sarah nodded sheepishly. "I promise, I'm not two-faced," she added.

She gave a little smile, mostly showing up in her green eyes, and kissed my forehead.

I realized Sarah didn't know my mood had changed from when she came into my room. She still treated me gently, and that's no longer what I wanted.

I scooted up and tilted my head to meet her lips with mine. At first our kiss was soft, gentle, sweet. As though our lips were meeting for the first time. But within breaths, it was as though we carried an unknown hunger for one another that only now burst free.

I slid my tongue into her mouth, and she responded with a groan. She cupped the back of my neck with her wide grip. Our tongues pushed deeper into one another's mouths, as though we couldn't get close enough, we couldn't taste each other enough.

My hands acted like ravenous beasts, looking for a meal, stalking up and down her back, grabbing and squeezing and grabbing some more. Her hips were thick and curvy, her back strong and wide. My tongue, suddenly jealous of my fingers, wanted every inch of her. She moaned with my touch as my left hand made its way down her belly, found the hem of her cotton T-shirt, and climbed up to cup a breast over her sports bra.

Goddess, I wanted her so badly.

She timidly ventured a hand under my shirt and found my naked breasts. She let out a moan and pulled my shirt up, revealing my nipples.

Goddess, I yearned for her mouth on them. I wanted her breasts in my mouth too, wanted to see her skin, her areolas, her nipples, all of her. But as I eased her shirt up, I felt her energy shift and took that as a no. My hands found the waistband to her flannel pajama pants, and this time her energy didn't have to stop me. She let loose of my breast to thwart my curious hand.

"Sorry," she whispered between kisses.

"No," I half said, half moaned. I leaned my chin back for her to access my neck. "No apology needed."

She pulled my shirt, previously bunched up above my breasts, over my head and tossed it to the end of the bed. Her mouth slowly descended on my left nipple, and I arched my back to give her more. My thighs squeezed. My pulse pounded in my ears.

Her mouth eased to the center of my chest and lingered before tracing down one of the lines of my abs with her tongue. When she grabbed at the waist of my pajama pants, I squirmed and shimmied to get them off faster. I needed her.

Now.

As though we spoke the same unsaid language, Sarah tossed my pj pants, panties, and all to the floor and buried her face between my legs.

I spread wider for her as she lapped me up with a gentle, wide pressed tongue.

Her tongue narrowed before she moved into smaller, quicker movements.

"Oh Goddess," I moaned, not able to spread my legs wide enough, not able to give her enough of myself.

My hips began to gyrate with pleasure. She wrapped her forearms around my thighs and kept me from escaping, kept me in her pleasure until I could stand it no longer and screamed out in absolute ecstasy.

Her head moved with the throbbing of my hips, as the pleasure rolled through me time and time again.

Sarah

I had never been with a woman, not really, until this moment. It had never felt right before. Of course, I'd stepped into a gay bar or two in Seattle. I'd kissed other women, but it never felt right to go further.

Despite my upbringing—basically everything I'd been taught about womankind tagged us as inferior to men—I had a reverence for women, a certain respect. So without a spark, or some kind of feelings for a woman I had kissed, I didn't feel it would be respectful to go further.

With Oriana, everything felt right. Her softness, her warmth, her wetness, her taste. God, I loved her taste.

I had heard my Hunter cousins talk about women when they didn't know I was listening. They'd call women's scents and tastes names, make jokes. Now I saw they diminished the power of what was between women's legs.

Of what was between Oriana's legs.

Her thighs, soft and squishy and strong, pulsed in rhythm when her moans were barely out of her mouth, and I adored it. Giving her pleasure gave me pleasure. I couldn't get enough.

After orgasming for the third time, she closed her legs on the sides of my head and giggled. "Okay, okay!"

I pulled away to kiss the tops of her thighs and smiled at her. I couldn't wait to hear her giggle like that again, my face between her legs.

She cupped my cheeks and led my lips to hers. She scooted out from under me and got on top to straddle.

I laughed.

"What are you doing?" I asked, my voice throaty and my tongue eager for more.

She only smiled and went to work on my pants. I allowed her to remove my pajama bottoms, but each inch they lowered, a new layer of anxiety grew within me.

Exposed, only in my underwear, Oriana kissed my stomach tenderly and played with the band of my boxers, sneaking her tongue between the tight fabric and my skin.

I tried. I tried to lean back and enjoy it. I wanted her, I wanted her lips on me, but I couldn't. It was like a wall blocking me from enjoying myself, and I couldn't see a way over it or through it.

It just was.

I cleared my throat and moved my hands from her back to the waistband of my underwear, restricting her access.

She stopped. "What's wrong?" she asked.

"Nothing," I muttered.

"Don't lie to a witch," she answered, her flirtatious grin gone from her face.

I couldn't tell if I'd ruined the moment or not.

I knew there was a reason I didn't want her lips and fingers below my navel, but the words explaining what I was feeling refused to show themselves—I couldn't explain anything past "I've never done that before."

Although I'd never gone down on a woman before tonight, and I didn't seem to have an issue with that.

Oriana's lips curved into the tiniest smile and my heart gave a little leap of joy. I hadn't ruined the moment. She nodded. "This must be a lot, to have someone you basically just met share a first sexual experience with you."

I kept silent because words seemed to be lodged in my mind, as hard as my heart pumped to dispel them and move on from the awkwardness now surrounding the two of us in her bed.

She placed her arms on either side of me and pulled herself up until her face hovered over mine. She kissed my forehead. "I want to connect with you," she whispered.

"Okay," I said, the words still not coming. I had no idea what she meant, but at the moment I wasn't sure I cared as long as she was kissing me. As long as she was happy and beside me.

"Can I take your boxers off?" she asked, and I couldn't help but give her adorable eagerness a nod. I tried to focus on her and not the pounding of my heart or the panic in my gut. She kept her eyes trained on mine as she lowered her torso and slowly eased my boxers from my waist. I lifted slightly to get them off my butt, and she tossed them from the bed.

She closed my legs and positioned her center on top of mine. Her hunger returned as she kissed my mouth, my neck, back up to my lips, and rocked her hips back and forth, back and forth, grinding softly, slowly, ever so intentionally.

My muscles tremored.

Warm wetness flooded where our bodies met. She moved faster, rocked deeper. My fingers dug into her back. My mouth opened, panting for more air.

She kissed my collarbone and rocked back and forth, back and forth, grinding her hips in a seductive dance for two, pulling my pleasure to the forefront, calling it forth.

Whimpers escaped my mouth.

Like a roller coaster climbing, climbing, climbing within me, she rocked and swayed and circled her hips until my mouth opened and my neck snapped back. My muscles tightened, and just in time, I clamped my mouth shut to keep from yelling out, as waves of the best feeling in the world rolled through me, became a part of me, and swept me up in their powerful pull.

"Oriana…" I exhaled once I was able to catch some semblance of a breath. The flashes of eroticism quieted into the warm, slow pulsing of pure connection. She slowed to a still and kissed my neck and mouth.

I squeezed her into me until she fell onto my chest and lay on top of my tingling body.

Waves of something more than pleasure rolled through my limbs. Connecting?

I flinched in pain under Oriana's weight, and she hurried to crawl off me. She sat beside me, her torso and face leaning over my midsection, pointed toward my face.

"Was I too heavy?" she asked, her voice no longer husky and low.

I tried to push myself up to ease her worry, but the tendons down my lower back and thighs clamped down, tightening, holding me into place. I clenched my fists and gritted my teeth.

"Oh Goddess." Oriana exhaled before jumping up and backing away. "Am I hurting you?"

I started to laugh at her absurdity, when another wave of tightness pulled at my lower back. "It's not you," I managed to get out. "I don't know."

God, my body was ruining it for me. Again.

Oriana set my pj bottoms on the bed and pulled her own on. Once dressed, she paced the side of the bed, watching me intently as though I'd combust at any moment.

For half a second, I wondered if she was causing this and if that meant there was a possibility I'd combust. But something deep inside, a knowing, kept my mind from wandering too far into old life thinking.

"Everything…just…got…tight." I managed to work the words from my lips rather than groaning or hissing.

"Do you need me to massage?" she asked, her hands barely touching my skin by the time she finished the sentence.

I sucked in a breath at her touch, and she jumped back. It was as though the closer she got to me, the closer our bodies physically came to one another, the stronger the pull of my muscles, as though they would tear from my skin and embrace her if they could. It was a gruesome picture, but one my mind kept replaying as though all of me yearned for exactly that.

For exactly her.

Oriana closed her eyes and muttered words under her breath, pleading words from the sound of it.

I inhaled a little deeper, my lungs accepting slightly more oxygen than moments before, and my muscles loosened enough for a deeper breath after that. "I just"—deep breath—"need to"—deep breath—"breathe."

With each inhale my body greedily accepted the oxygen and, in turn, released my constricted muscles just slightly.

"Like this," Oriana said, sitting on the bed beside me in the dark, our clothes littering the bedroom floor. She started sketching in the air the first two sides of a square.

"In for five," she said as she drew her finger down an invisible line.

"And hold for five." She drew a horizontal line. "Exhale for five," she continued as she drew a third line. She drew the fourth line. "Now hold for five more."

After five breaths my hands unclutched. After seven breaths my teeth unclenched.

I finally breathed out on a deep exhale and flashed Oriana a smile. "Thank you."

"For what?" she asked, her head tilted in confusion.

"For whatever spell you just said under your breath," I answered. "It's getting better. The pain is not so intense."

She shook her head, her dark, gorgeous hair messy in the sexiest way from our intimacy.

Her hair, so much longer and more wild than my own. I smiled.

I felt my mind capable of thought again, outside of the shock of sudden pain.

"I was calling to my auntie's ghost," Oriana stated, her eyes wide with a new kind of concern that painted itself differently than the concern for me she'd worn only minutes earlier. "She's not here."

Oriana peered around her bedroom. "She never ignores me, so it can't be that."

I didn't have it in me to pry further, to ask what she thought this could mean. And how long had her auntie's ghost been in her place, and was an old dead lady watching me?

Did she see me pee?

I chuckled to myself at the thought of asking such an asinine question. Although I still wanted to know.

"It's not funny," Oriana exclaimed, her brows low and serious.

"No," I tried to assure her, "I'm not laughing at that."

But Oriana's mind was too lost in thought to register my half explanation. "I don't know if something happened to her," she trailed off.

I tried to sit up on her bed, to open my arms and tell her to climb on in and I'd comfort her, we'd figure out her missing dead aunt's ghost together. But whatever was messing with my lower back must have irritated my sciatic nerve, shooting pain down my right leg.

"Fuck," I hissed and froze, unwilling to endure what it would take to move again.

"This isn't right," Oriana seemed to say to herself as she snatched her phone from her nightstand. "Something isn't right. I can feel it. An energy has changed. It's not right."

I shoved myself up in bed, ignoring the screaming sciatica. She needed me, and damn if I wasn't going to rise to the occasion—literally. As much as it pained me, I opened my arms.

Within a breath she unlocked her phone. She ignored my nonverbal invitation. "I need to let the coven know if they don't already," she explained without looking at me. "They haven't texted or called me. Why haven't they? If they felt it, they should have…"

Oriana's eyes shot open and her chest raised slowly, then fell hard. She only stared at her screen, only clutched the cell phone. Her breaths grew shallow.

"What?" I asked, wishing I could leap from the bed and catch her up in my arms, show her she was safe and secure with me, despite which ghosts might or might not be present. But I doubted I would be able to jump out without toppling over and taking her with me to the floor. "Is it your coven? Did they message you?"

She shook her head, still staring at her screen. Her face twisted and her hands began to shake. She swallowed hard.

I took a deep breath and slowly maneuvered myself to the edge of the bed. Another breath and I was up, standing in front of her, the phone between the both of us.

The text Oriana had been entranced by didn't have an actual contact name. Just a random cell phone number her phone didn't seem to recognize.

But the words in the text...those had to be from her ex. He must have gotten ahold of a different phone, one I hadn't blocked.

I didn't know how I knew, but I knew. It was as though I could feel her confusion shift to fear. Weakness washed over her.

How could I feel this? How could I feel what she felt?

The questions dropped from my mind. Yes, I *knew*. Who else would send a text this late at night in the middle of the week? Who else would have the audacity?

We both stared at the screen, and suddenly my confusion over what had been happening to me, why I'd felt the intense pain after making love to Oriana, and it *was* making love, made sense.

It had to be. What else could cause the muscle pain and sudden rage?

The witch had woken my inner Hunter. That part of me that wasn't supposed to exist because I was a woman. The old world Hunter, created by the monks to eradicate witches and Wild Women.

My Hunter had claimed the witch as mate.

Oriana's chin rose, and for the first time since she muttered those words to her dead aunt's ghost, she gazed into my eyes.

Only this Oriana was scared, timid, and on the verge of crying. Her eyes filled with tears, pleading. Her focus jerked to look out her window from where we stood, and then back to me.

I caught her gaze to reassure her, but I couldn't be sure that was what my eyes were expressing. Because that's not at all what I felt. Hot rage, searing anger, and a need to kill is what I felt.

My Hunter chose her mate.

My Hunter refused to allow her mate to fear anyone, least of all a poor excuse for a human male. I peered back down at her phone.

I'm here to talk, the text from the random number said. *Come outside.*

And just like that, every ounce of pain that pulled and twisted my muscles vanished.

My Hunter smiled.

And so did I.

CHAPTER THIRTEEN

Oriana

I couldn't run fast enough. Couldn't get enough crisp night air in my lungs to slow my wildly beating heart and calm my fears.

But hadn't I had the fears for a reason? Hadn't I learned Steven was capable of anything? Or everything? He had already shown me how his brain worked, his serious lack of empathy coupled with an inflated sense of entitlement. Without empathy, and with the belief all is owed to you, a person could do anything and everything.

"He's a human," I reminded myself before throwing the back door open and scuttering down the back steps. I wanted to surprise him by coming from the back. Wanted to show I'm not easily scared.

Though I vibrated like an excited chihuahua.

I nearly zoomed around the side of my mobile before I paused to take a breath.

Ground. I needed to ground. Couldn't let my anxiety push me into a situation I wasn't prepared to handle. And when it came to Steven, I could never be prepared enough.

My legs shook, and I grabbed the siding of my home for stability. *Breathe*.

I forced myself to slow my breaths, to imagine roots growing from the soles of my feet like those of the dark evergreens towering above me. But the ever-scratching paw of anxiety only dug its claws deeper. I hated this. I hated how even after our divorce, he got to choose when and where to scare the shit out of me. He got to decide when we'd interact, even if it meant in the middle of the night. I loathed the fact that everything was on his terms.

"She didn't answer my calls or my texts!" I heard a male voice whine from my driveway.

"Fuck your calls and texts," Sarah yelled from the front of my house, her voice low and booming with strength, a tone I'd never heard from her but felt drawn to in a nervous kind of way. "Did you consider she *declined* your calls and texts because she wants nothing to do with you?"

I froze, clinging to the side of my house in the dark.

I'd pay for this, for Sarah's honesty. She had no idea the storm her words were conjuring. Telling someone who was incapable of realizing others had feelings and needs of their own. He'd only take offense. There was no other option.

Honesty was vulnerability, and my vulnerabilities were his playthings, his tools to get what he wanted, no matter how he had to wield them.

Silence hung in the air around my home. Even the nocturnal animals paused to listen.

"And what?" he countered too late to make it impactful. "Now you're gonna try to tell me she knows what's best?" He laughed. "Have you had to actually live with her?"

My legs quivered. My chest tightened. I slouched against my home. Sarah had no idea how much I questioned myself, how I didn't trust my own thoughts and feelings half the time.

No one knew.

Except maybe my ex-husband. And he was standing there, standing where there would soon be gravel for a driveway, revealing my hidden truths to the woman I couldn't get out of my heart and head. Shining a heat lamp onto the fact that I wasn't the strong, confident witch I showed off to the world, to Sarah, to the other Wild Women.

I was a new witch.

A weak witch.

A questioning witch.

A scared woman.

Not the proud, all-knowing woman of the woods a Wild could respect and love. I had been walking around, fractured pieces melded together. Each word I allowed him to say was a revelation to Sarah that tapped the barely held-together pieces of me.

I inhaled and slowly exhaled, seconds away from shattering. Drops of rain sprayed from my lips. The motion light in my front yard seemed almost trained on Steven. The breath from his words twisted in the mist as it rose toward the light.

"She acts like she has it all together, but unless you've lived with her like me, you wouldn't know it's all fake," he continued, as though he was talking to a buddy.

As though he expected her to totally understand what he was saying and even feel badly for him. That she would finally understand his plight.

Would she, though?

Shame somehow had a way of bubbling to the surface with the weight of drowning certainty.

I flipped through an inner Rolodex of past mistakes and winced. I couldn't let him say any more. I moved to step away from the side of the house, into view of Steven and Sarah in the front, but embarrassment welded me in place.

"What are you even talking about?" Sarah said, the sneer in her voice clear without seeing her face.

I clung to the fake wood siding, barely able to see Steven's back leg as he shifted in the mud.

I looked down to my own bare feet, mud squished between my toes. I had forgotten boots.

"She's not right in the head," Steven started as he moved out of my line of sight and closer to my front porch. Closer to Sarah.

For less than a second I wondered how a huldra like Sarah would teach a man like Steven a lesson. The thought didn't last long enough for it to bring a smile to my face.

"I think..." Sarah started to say and abruptly stopped. "No, I know it's time for you to get back into whatever little car you came in, and head back home. It's late. Leave." A rumble lived at the foundation of the last word, *leave*. It sounded like a threat.

I peered around the side corner of my house. I took another step, outing my presence.

Neither noticed me, their eyes too locked on the other. Well, his focus seemed on Sarah as a whole. Sarah's eyes stayed trained on his hands and eyes.

I looked for Steven's minicab truck, but he hadn't driven one up to my house.

Steven put his hands on his hips and turned to look down the driveway, down the hill. "Little?" he asked. He turned back toward Sarah standing on the small porch, him on the ground, drizzle snaking down his slightly confused face.

Did he park at the bottom of the hill and walk up? Why?

"Leave," is all she said. This time the growl in her voice made itself very clear.

"Yes, Steven," I said, making my presence known, and feeling an ounce of confidence at Sarah's Wild Woman growl. "I do not want you on *my* property. So you can leave now."

I shot a look to Sarah, who still stared at Steven, but now with a smirk.

Steven masked his initial shock within seconds of letting his true self slip into view. But I saw it. I saw the quick flash of shock and fear and hurt. His true emotions never lasted long before his mask fit itself securely into place.

Now disdain covered his face as he shook his head knowingly and sighed. "She gets like this," he said to Sarah as though he was talking about a small child. "Once she gets this way, it's hard reasoning with her. She can't think straight, or even logically."

Nothing about Sarah's appearance shifted toward understanding of him, toward putting the puzzle pieces in place to realize I was who Steven said I was: a broken, chaotic, depressed child of a woman who needed...who just needed.

But I couldn't help worrying that his words were hitting somewhere inside, a recollection of some sort that, yes, she had noticed the way I flew off the handle when I was overwhelmed, like a small child unable to cope with reality.

I did prefer the unseen parts of our world, what Steven regarded as make-believe and made me incapable of reason or logic.

"You are not welcome here," Sarah boomed, as though she had waited, considered, and decided.

Had she decided Steven was mentally unstable...or me?

No, she had seen reason. Hadn't she?

It was so hard to know these days. When I was younger, before Steven, I had been so sure of things, of people and outcomes. Now... now I wasn't sure. I couldn't be sure. Not when I tended to be wrong about people, to trust aspects of them, of myself, that didn't exist.

"Take another step toward her," Sarah warned, her Wild Woman shining through her eyes. I could see that, a being hiding in the human facade, eager to pounce, warning for the right reasons. "It'll be your last."

I blinked, and despite the fact that I had already been watching her, Sarah's presence demanded I watch closer still. A rock in the sea, a safe place to rest. That's what I saw.

Mentally, I clung to her. Like a starfish lost at sea, I gravitated toward her until I stood in the mud directly in front of the small front porch she stood upon. I could trust this Wild Woman, who, like me, believed in the unseen, *lived* in the unseen. No matter how Steven shook my self-resolve and eroded my sense of independence, Sarah knew better.

Sarah gave me strength.

And hope.

In a way, Sarah gave me a leg to stand on.

"You can leave now," I announced, standing firmly now in my resolve. "You don't belong here. You can't just come to my house. It doesn't work like that. The papers are filed—we're done. You don't get to just show up anymore." My decrees, because that's what they felt like, came swiftly and surely. "You don't get to just call when you feel like fucking with my head."

His expression twisted in confusion. "Fucking with your head?" he asked, almost earnestly, if it wasn't for the sliver of condemnation in his voice. "Whose insurance allowed you to see the best therapists, as much as you needed?" He waited. "Mine. I've only ever supported you, your career, your healing."

"Yeah," I scoffed, feeling more grounded and confrontational with him than I had in a long time. "On the outside you were the best. But we both know the truth."

How he had bashed me at parties when he'd had too much to drink, which was every time. *She's working through some things*, he'd tell complete strangers, as though he was only trying to protect my reputation. As though I was ruining it and he was coming along behind me, doing damage control.

How he had urged me to pursue my career dreams in one breath and complained that I put my dreams above him on the next breath.

How he had suggested I take the yoga trainer course to be certified, but each time the joint checking account ran low it was because I spent too much money on myself.

His confused expression fell into understanding. He nodded with a smile that didn't show his teeth or touch his brown eyes. "We do know the truth," he answered solemnly.

My shoulders dropped from beside my ears.

As though he had given up, as though he was ready to turn and head down the hill, off my property and out of my life, he pulled car keys from his pocket and gave an understanding nod to no one.

He sighed. "I guess I came up here hoping for the woman I fell in love with."

His statement hit me from the side and knocked me for a mental loop. It was one I had heard many times before.

When we were alone, his statement would be followed by all the ways I had changed, all the ways I had baited and switched him. How he'd been the one in the couple to draw the short stick, having to fall in love with a woman mentally deranged and unstable with finances, relationships, and work.

I didn't know if it was Sarah's presence behind me, above me, that gave me what I felt, in the moment, as permission. It could have been much simpler than that. It could have been just good ol' fashioned rage. But the moment my tongue massaged the second word from my mouth, I was barreling toward him.

"I'm not crazy!" I screamed.

His arms shot up over his face, as though he had to protect himself, as though we'd done this before and he knew the position.

But we hadn't done it before. We hadn't ever played out a scenario where I fought back to this degree, where I lost it and he just lost.

His self-protection was grossly overdone. I didn't go for his face with my nails. Didn't throw a fist to his gut. I only shoved him, my flat hands on his chest, my eyes burning with wetness.

The words *get out* didn't have time to form, to be screeched at this trespasser, when he wrapped his strong hands around each of my wrists and twisted.

I hadn't seen it coming. Hadn't braced myself to twist out of his arms and away.

The shock of pain took me to my knees in the mud before Steven. His judgmental eyes leered down at me, reminding me of my place, beneath him.

But they only stayed trained on me for mere seconds before commotion shot his gaze up and painted terror across his face.

I didn't have time to turn to see what Steven saw. Sarah leaped over me, her hands firmly on Steven's shoulders, and tackled him to the ground. His back and head hit the mud, but he didn't dare get up with a Wild Woman crouched over his midsection.

He lay still, his eyes staring up at her. He said nothing, only stared, as though he was processing how he ended up on the ground.

She turned to me, while using her arms and legs to hold down Steven's extremities.

I stayed crouched low to the ground. I felt the presence of a soul, of my resident witch ghost, but it was as though a veil shifted between her reality and mine. I couldn't hear her, couldn't see her. I felt enough to know she was trying to tell me something, but my awareness wouldn't allow her words to penetrate my understanding.

"I said *stay down*," Sarah yelled, holding Steven in the mud.

I peered up, hoping to find my coven foremother hovering, hoping that's who I felt. But nothing.

As happens in the early morning hours of a western Washington spring, a heavy mist began to nestle into the tops of trees around us, releasing a dampness that had always reminded me of a soft blanket of little full clouds.

A soft, comforting blanket from nature to me.

I watched as Sarah held Steven down, as though she waited for him to stop fighting her, just to show him it was no use.

This Wild Woman had protected me, stood up for my honor, trusted that I was to be defended and he was the one in the wrong. Not me. My coven sisters had supported me, of course, but they had never come into contact with him.

My gaze slowly shifted from the foggy treetops to the Wild Woman. I gave a lazy smile, my heart and mind validated, a sense of magic resting upon my heart.

Sarah's eyes softened when she regarded me. *You okay?* she mouthed.

My smile didn't waver. I was okay. With her, I'd be okay. Very okay.

"You okay to go inside?" This time she spoke audibly, still hovering over Steven.

I didn't ask why, didn't question why she'd want me inside as she stayed outside. My protector was protecting, a sensation I couldn't remember feeling before.

I nodded and pulled myself from the mud. A little dirt never bothered me. Still, once I stood I wiped my wet and muddy hands on my pj pants and absently made my way inside to change.

I should get Sarah dry sweats to wear, I thought. When she comes back in.

Sarah and Steven kept in place as I walked up my front steps and into my home. I shut the door behind me, wiped my feet on the entry rug, and padded to my gas fireplace to flip the switch.

The warmth of instant fire would do well to thaw my tense muscles. I couldn't wait for Sarah to come in, to walk over to me and wrap her arms around me, and lie on the floor in front of the fire with me.

I was grabbing a blanket when Faline and Shawna appeared in my hallway.

"What's going on out there?" Shawna asked.

"It's all right," I assured the two. "Sarah is handling it."

Faline peered out the large front windows.

"Didn't you guys hear everything?" I asked, not totally ignorant to the Wild Women's abilities. At least theirs.

"That's the problem," Shawna answered. "We did." She sat on my couch, watching Faline, who stood at the front window.

"How's that a problem?" I said.

My answer didn't come from Faline's or Shawna's lips. It came in the sound of a thud.

I shot up to peer out the windows, to see Sarah holding Steven up, his feet dangling above the ground.

"Fuck," Faline breathed out. She balled her fists and pulled her top lip in as she took a deep breath. "This isn't good."

"If you go out there," Shawna said, her voice low and warning and serious, "you'll only activate her more. Our presence will only make her worse."

Faline shot Shawna a sharp and knowing look. "I know." She exhaled. With her arm straight, she leaned a hand on the window frame like the thing held her back.

My heart felt like it was flung from my chest and hit the floor with the weight of what played out before my eyes.

My Wild Woman, Sarah, gripped the collar of Steven's jacket, dragging him through the mud, toward the trees, the forest. Her short-sleeve shirt revealed muscles, swollen and tight. Tattoos that hadn't been there moments earlier etched new, dark lines across her skin before my eyes.

I blinked. It couldn't be true. It couldn't.

But it was true.

Either from anger or sadness or maybe both, the tears I'd held back until now began to escape.

How dared she.

How dared she lie to me, let me think she was someone she wasn't.

A fresh anger burned within me and demanded I seek justice. I bolted to the front door. Faline reached an arm to block me, but I pivoted and spun around her, thrusting the door open.

"Hunter!" was all I could screech into the misty early morning before Shawna wrapped a strong arm around my waist, pulled me back, and slammed the door.

CHAPTER FOURTEEN

Sarah

My body burned and ached, the way one does after a rigorous workout. Except my muscles weren't spent. They were growing.

My forearms and biceps shook, almost vibrated, swelling.

"For trespassing," I heard myself grind out, but in an angry, seething voice that was not my own, "you have forfeited your vehicle to Oriana."

A bolt of pain ripped through my right arm, the arm I dragged Steven through the mud and pine needles with. His shoes trailed furrows behind us. I nearly released him but held on just long enough for the wave to wash over me. "As payment for pain and suffering."

A fresh tattoo finished etching itself into the front of my right forearm. Nonstop bolts of pain accompanied it.

I pushed past the pain. I had to get this poor excuse for a man down this hill and off Oriana's property. He had stopped struggling once we passed the tree line and made it deeper into the woods. Now he pathetically whimpered his innocence. His limbs dragged in the dirt, leaving divots in the mud. He looked like a disheveled rag doll, head hanging, mouth uttering about the trouble Oriana had brought into his life.

His complaints, which sounded more like pleas, fell on deaf ears.

A quarter of a mile down the hill and his whiny, poor-me voice started grating on my nerves. I imagined picking him up and flinging him into a tree. That would shut him up.

"You are not worthy of life," I heard myself say as an affirmation, preparing to throw him out like waste and be done with him.

I froze. *Done with him?* When had I ever thought murder was the answer? When had I ever been so flippant about life? About another living being?

Steven looked up at me, his eyes red and swollen. His legs hung, bent at the knees, the toes of his tennis shoes caked in mud. "Are you going to let me go now?" he asked, or more like begged.

I didn't want to let him go. I couldn't even consider that option. My brain wanted punishment. It wanted death coupled with excruciating pain.

A flood of pure, blue-hot rage swept through me, and it was all I could do to open my hands, release my grip on Steven, before I did what I wanted, before I raised him high into the air and flung his body at the nearest and thickest tree trunk. Until I watched his weak spine hit the bark and contort in inhuman ways.

Oriana flashed into my mind, into my heart. I couldn't. For her, I couldn't.

Mine.

"She's mine," I growled out to Steven.

The desire to kill him doubled and folded in on itself, growing stronger with each breath. "Mine," I think I repeated, because Steven answered.

"Fine, she's yours," he whined. "You can have her."

Black lines swirled on the top of my right hand, the hand I held Steven's coat collar with. My skin burned, and I released him to fall backward into the mud. He stayed down and only peered up at me, waiting.

The sun was trying to come up, behind thick layers of cloud cover. The twilight of early morning revealed tear streaks down his cheeks. Yesterday, I would never have allowed this to get so far, never would have taken any type of delight in making this man fear for his life.

Now it seemed his terror fed my anger, my strength, my desire for power.

My father flashed through my mind, his large hand on the back of my neck, squeezing a silent directive, causing me to feel small and insignificant. And scared.

Was this what my Hunter brothers went through? Was this why

we were separated from them from puberty and on? Did they feel this rage too? Did they lose control the first time their Hunter truly showed itself and took over too?

"Go," I ground out.

A tiny part of myself was still in control, still wanted to stay in control, though I couldn't be sure how long that part would hold on. My Hunter wasn't taking no for an answer as she tore through me, claimed me, her smile wide and her hands bloody.

I peered down at my hands, expecting blood, as my vision blurred.

Words that were not mine ripped from my throat. "She's coming!" I screamed into the night. My Hunter celebrated for a name I had never heard of before.

"Who?" my captive yelled back from the ground beneath me, his terror holding him in place. He finally seemed to realize the danger and scrambled backward like a crab, his hands pushing through dead leaves and mud. Evergreens towered above, creating shadows of the moonlight among the skeletons of leafless alders.

Staying low, Steven scurried to an evergreen trunk for safety.

My thudding heart stilled. The tearing sensations in my muscles broke free. The pain of new tattoos etching themselves along my skin calmed and vanished. I stood, a pillar of a woman, and raised my eyes to meet Steven's. He clung to the tree trunk and pulled himself up to stand, hiding behind the thing like it was an iron shield. Or maybe he hoped it would be.

I licked my lips and cracked my knuckles. But it wasn't me, it was a version of me who took control and made everything okay. Made everything simple. Made it all painless.

I felt a slow smile grow upon my face, pulling my lips wide and tight. "She's here."

Steven backed up. His shoes caught on a fern, but he quickly righted himself until his back hit another evergreen. His dark coat was torn all over, shreds of it falling loose. Drying mud caked at his elbows and knees.

"Who?" he yelled out in fear, frantically looking around in the dark morning, as if he could see if someone approached.

I almost laughed at his absurdity. "Brigid is here," I said easily, casually.

And it was casual, the way it felt as though this new energy tried me on, as though it was wrapping itself around me, my hooded cape for the job ahead. Had I stepped back so my Hunter could step forward? A tiny voice deep in the abyss of me whispered this question. I didn't think on it, though, didn't try to conjure up an answer. It didn't matter. This new power felt amazing, buzzed under my skin in the most magnificent way.

It wasn't me who took note of every movement, every eye twitch of my prey, of the vile monster I now hunted. It was my Hunter. "You have sinned," I started, speaking through a smile. "Fear not. Your blood will redeem you."

Power, intent, and a deep belonging coursed through my muscles, fed them, as though the belonging to my family, the type I had longed for my whole life, suddenly washed away my transgressions against them and deemed me worthy.

My calves tingled with strength and anticipation.

One step in his direction was all it took. He screamed, spun around, and fled deeper into the woods, down the hill. I walked, following him, allowing him time to think about what he had done before exacting his punishment.

His terror excited me, sent shivers through me.

He knew his sin. He knew what he deserved as penance.

"God is love," I recited loudly for the wicked sinner I sought. "Love requires empathy."

My boots securely traversed the woods. My Hunter Brigid knew how to locate the human male...*I* knew how to locate him. His sin glowed in the darkness, but not in the light weightless glow of holiness. No, Steven emanated a swirl of inky darkness, a void so deep that what glowed were the areas around it, the night around him.

Steven's soul was darker than the dark. God required his death at my hands. And as God's faithful servant, I was more than pleased to obey.

With Brigid in control, scents were stronger and energy showed itself. His cloud of darkness moved quickly, but not quick enough. I picked up my pace to a trot, my strong legs pushing me forward through the wet, dead underbrush. With each footfall I picked up speed, ready to exile this evil soul from the human plane of existence.

I felt for my dagger at my hip, but my hands touched nothing other than sweats. I looked down as I ran. The absence of a dagger felt wrong. How would I properly eradicate such a dark soul without the dagger? I patted my chest, my thighs…it had to be on me.

Hunters always wore their holy-forged daggers, complete with a particular red stone that brought weakness to Wild Women before the blade gave them death.

The moment I bent my body at my waist, just enough to look down to my feet, to check for a dagger strapped to my ankle, something pounced from the limbs of a nearby evergreen and wrestled me to the ground.

I fought it off, *her* off, and flung her to the trunk of a tree like the pest she was. Unlike the human, she twisted in enough time to clasp onto the bark and scurry up, to hide in the branches. Then another force hit me from behind and tackled me to the ground.

"Evil!" I yelled before shoving myself from the ground and catapulting the second woman from my back.

She jumped back and squatted close to the ground, as though she was waiting to pounce on me again.

"Sarah," another woman's voice said. "Sarah, come back."

I shot a glare up the tree branch. A huldra perched away from the trunk, steady.

"God shall cleanse you from your sins," I announced, an automatic phrase that felt more real, more sure than I'd felt about anything in a long time.

"You don't have a dagger," she said from the tree.

I looked down to see my hand searching for a blade.

I remembered my prey, the dark soul I chased, and sprinted toward him. The first Wild Woman, the one with braids, bounded up into an evergreen I ran toward.

I halted.

"Let him go," she said. "You've done enough for your mate."

My mate.

"Mine!" I yelled to the huldra. Something in me, at the edge of my understanding, recognized these Wilds as unsafe.

The other Wild Woman jumped from her tree to the first one's tree. They stood above me, out of my reach. "Sarah," she said, "Oriana is safe. You can stop now."

I glowered into their eyes, but they didn't return my hate with a brand of their own. Their expressions seemed concerned, tired. Not deadly, not hate-filled.

"Oriana," I uttered. "My Oriana."

"Yes," the woman assured me. "And I am Faline, and this is Shawna." She regarded the huldra beside her. "We're Oriana's friends. And we're your family. You're letting your Hunter take over, and you've got to come back."

"My mate?" I asked. Memories trickled into my mind of holding her, touching her smooth skin, feeling her soft lips on mine. Her thighs. My heart pulsed.

"Yes, Sarah," Faline said.

"Brigid," I corrected her. "Saint Brigid."

"No, your name is Sarah," Faline said slowly and calmly. "Brigid is your Hunter, and you can't let her control you. You can't let her make decisions for you."

When I didn't move, she said, "Do you remember Marcus?"

Knowing and comfort and home flooded my mind. My Hunter brother.

"Okay, that hit," she said, but not to me.

"Do you want to talk to Marcus? Maybe let him clear up a few things?" she asked.

I blinked and held my eyes closed for a breath. "I want Oriana." My tattoos had stopped swirling and creating themselves, stopped etching their reliefs into my skin, and I suddenly noticed the brilliance they left behind.

A large thick black cross covered the inside of my right forearm. The image of my childhood, of the Hunter Brotherhood, of everything that stood for my oppression, was now inked permanently onto my skin.

I groaned and my shoulders fell. I woke from a nightmare to see me as the monster. My knees gave out, and I let go to fall backward into the decomposing forest floor.

I never wanted to get up or show my face again. "Just let me die here," I said on an exhale. Tears filled my eyes.

Faline came closer and crouched in front of me. "Sarah? You back?"

I couldn't meet her eyes. In the last few years, especially, but all my life I had known hopelessness. The emotion or feeling or whatever it is was like an old friend who often dropped by unannounced and left me thinking my life was pointless.

But now, as I sat on the wet forest floor in the early morning darkness, I wished the light of day would not come. I was an ex-Hunter who never was accepted as one, now with an obvious mark on my body proclaiming this exact heritage. I was hated by my own kind and by the enemies of my kind.

Every mature Hunter male I grew up around had some rendition of a cross tattooed on his forearm. Now I did too. I already knew it would be a daily reminder that I was, and always would be, an outcast.

"Do you want me to call Marcus?" Faline asked gently.

I only stared at my right forearm, turning and twisting to take in the ink's intricacy and beauty. Each line bled into the other, forming what looked like a metal cross. I had seen male Hunters with tattoos and heard them talk about the pain of man-made tattoos versus the pain of God-given tattoos. That's what they had called them, God-given. Now I knew. I was marked by God, and no amount of unwillingness or defiance could change my fate.

I looked up at Faline, desperation in my heart. "Why would a God who doesn't want me mark me?" I asked. It wasn't fair. None of this female Hunter stuff had been fair, but this especially.

"Oh, sweetie." Faline shifted, crouching closer, and leaned in to wrap her arms around my shoulders. I didn't hug her back. I didn't have it in me. "The tattoos arrive from an unlocking of abilities. They're a good thing."

She didn't look convinced, and I didn't blame her. "Hunter abilities?" I scoffed. "Like tracking down innocent women and killing them out of fear of their power?"

She had nothing for that.

I stood, causing her embrace to fall and release. She rose to meet my eyes.

"You ready to go back now?" she asked.

Shawna approached us, a sad smile lifting her expression only slightly. In her eyes, I saw softness, the type that comes from trauma and the subsequent healing from it. Trauma caused by Hunters. Hunters like me.

Wordlessly, the three of us tromped back to the house, over fallen branches and logs, drenched ferns, and half-dead blackberry brambles.

The huldra could have gotten back by a quicker route of leaping through evergreens, but they walked beside me.

When the lights of Oriana's home came into view, peeking through the evergreens and mist, I stopped.

The Wild Women noticed and turned toward me, lagging behind. I didn't give them a chance to say a word. I had made up my mind. "I'm not going in there with you. I only walked you to your temporary dwelling." The words were not my own, more serious, more guarded. Maybe they were the new me. The me that felt shattered inside, with the sharp cutting edges of a hopeless reality.

"Sarah," Faline pleaded softly, as though even her words walked on jagged eggshells. "Not every Hunter is led by such a powerful being as Brigid."

I only stared past her at the lit back window of Oriana's home. She had to be in her kitchen, probably whipping up something warm and delicious with Friday. They would be setting the table and inviting the Wild Women to enjoy a meal and laughter with them.

I would never be welcome to sit at Oriana's table again. Not with the obvious mark on my arm.

"But having the spirit of a notable priest to help is an honor," Faline continued. Her words weren't disingenuous, but they also didn't carry the pseudo-acceptance she tried to get me to feel. "As a woman, you received the help of Brigid. This is huge, Sarah. You're unlocking truths for your fellow female Hunters."

My gazed snapped back to Faline's face. Her red hair was pulled back in a ponytail and water droplets from the misty night snaked down her face.

"I know you're afraid, but please don't shut us out."

Afraid? I wanted to scoff.

Afraid didn't touch it.

I was becoming my ancestors, everything I hated, the very reasons I felt foreign in my own skin. And I was powerless to stop it. Yet again, powerless to stand against the Hunter establishment.

Faline and Shawna could fight the establishment and win because they weren't from it. It didn't pump through their veins with each heartbeat. It didn't permeate every thought, every fear, every joy. How could they ever understand? No one could.

I inhaled deep and long, and spoke on the exhale. "Please, do not come for me."

I spun around and bolted for the heart of the forest. I ran with a power I'd never felt before. Strength pulsated in my veins, spread through my muscles, with each tear, each rip of new growth.

The Wilds didn't follow me. And for their sake, I was glad.

CHAPTER FIFTEEN

Oriana

My body shook with fury as I glared out into the darkness of my property. If I had my way, I would have already placed an energy shield around my home and forgotten this ever happened. But Friday lay asleep in the guest room she shared with her mother. And Shawna had left my side to join Faline. When Shawna had run off after Faline, I assumed it was to go take down the Hunter—two Wild Women are more effective than one. But then I remembered they were friends, a team.

They had to have known Sarah was a Hunter.

Were they all in on this deception?

I couldn't let myself fall into the rabbit hole of paranoia. I couldn't place the blame on my new friends, on the people here to help me.

Sarah was the Hunter. She was the being on my land who didn't belong. A being whose muscles and bravery were forged with the oppression of others. A being whose abilities were made stronger by killing and malice. Killing innocent women, innocent witches.

How could she? Sarah knew my land was not welcoming to Hunters, that *I* was not welcoming to Hunters. And yet she paraded around, pretending to be a Wild Woman. Lying to me. She was bullshit. It was all bullshit.

She lied to help me.

No. Lies have no excuse, I reminded myself.

I had been down this path before. I had trusted the untrustworthy, the down on their luck. I had given excuses for deplorable behavior, in hopes my fantasies were more correct than their reality. In hopes that they truly did care for me, and it had all been a misunderstanding. In hopes that I would have someone, anyone, to love me.

I swore to myself I would never make excuses again for the way others treated me. I'd done the work, listened to and read great books on healing after narcissistic abuse. I knew the damaging effects of emotionally immature parents and how the adult child unknowingly seeks out emotionally immature or unavailable partners to recreate the twisted comfort they had growing up.

I was not going to allow myself to fall into that trap again, to ensnare myself in the past. I deserved real, true love.

I wiped my eyes and backed away from window to collapse on my couch.

I was a fool.

Yet again, I had started falling for someone who didn't deserve me, who met my honesty and vulnerability with deceit and manipulation. I pulled my cell from my pajama pocket and opened a thread of texts between Serene and me, my therapist coven sister, the one who had helped me see and heal so much of my heart.

I did it again, I texted and then realized the vagueness of my message. Especially at this time of the morning. *Sarah is a Hunter, not a Wild.*

It took a few breaths before the three little dots showed up. No doubt my insanely early morning text woke her.

Sarah, as in your crush? she texted back.

Not my crush anymore, I thought, but figured sending that would just be stating the obvious.

I left the openness of the living room and sought privacy in my room. I softly closed my bedroom door behind me and crawled under my comforter.

Alone, I went back to texting. My fingers flew over the screen. *Yeah, the Wilds brought Hunters to help with the build, and I sent all the Hunters away. Sarah stayed, so I assumed she was a Wild. But she's a Hunter.*

Hunters can be women?! she messaged back. *I had no idea!*

I paused to consider that Serene, a longtime coven sister whose energy-shifting abilities left me in awe, also didn't know such a thing could exist. If Hunter women weren't known to exist, but Sarah did, didn't that make her special?

No. It made her a Hunter.

It made her a liar. At least to me.

I was sure she was still special, like all people are. But the place she held in my heart, the home our private glances and energy sharing and long talks were creating...

She had taken a sledgehammer and smashed it to smithereens.

I hated her for that. I had started to truly hope again that I could actually find love, that someone could actually look at me, flaws and witchyness and all, and still adore me. Because I refused to accept anything less than adoration again.

It's just, I wasn't sure I could find adoration. And then Sarah came along and saw me.

I sighed and slunk deeper into my bed. I pulled the covers up to my neck and lay there, looking up at the ceiling. I couldn't remember ever being seen outside of one-to-one rituals, energy treatments and readings with my coven sisters. And even then, there was something life-altering about meeting a person who could see all of me, the way my coven sisters did, and then also find access to the deeper parts. The naked, vulnerable parts that no one saw.

I wanted Sarah to see those parts of me.

And fuck me, I still ached for it, for her.

I wouldn't listen to that ache, though. I knew it came from an unhealthy place inside me, a hurting child who desired love above all else. A lonely woman who had disconnected from herself so much that she didn't realize she was lonely.

I refused to betray myself for the facade of love. Never again.

Hunters were the reason witches were deemed evil, were hanged and burned and demonized. Sarah's ancestors caused that. The marks on her skin were a telltale sign. I'd never watched them appear in real time before her. I'd heard stories of them, and other coven members had been known to interact with a Hunter or two. Our foremothers had fought Hunters to keep the Obsidian Falls waterfall our own, and not hand it over to their corrupt and controlling ways.

They would have used the waterfall for their destructive magic and called it holy and righteous.

"I need your help, sister." I whispered into the dark for the old coven spirit who showed up the day the Hunters came. I felt frozen in uncertainty, and I needed her to tell me what to do next.

On my phone, Serene seemed more fascinated about Sarah than anything else. That's not what I needed. I needed support, someone who understood Sarah's betrayal.

I waited for a tingling across my forearm or at the back of my neck. I waited for the energy to shift, but it never did.

"Sister," I called, a little louder this time. "Why have you left me? Please."

Emptiness, the lack of response, and the sudden burst of loneliness collided, and I pulled the comforter over my head. Could I just lie here for the rest of my life? Trying to be strong, to push forward to build the life I wanted, was exhausting. It wasn't just planning and being responsible with a touch of imagination and vision. It included the daily trudging through hip-deep fear, old programming, and emotional exhaustion. It was a near-daily battle that had somehow gotten lighter, freer, more real when the Wilds showed up. When Sarah showed up.

I groaned inwardly. Of course that's like me—falling for a liar. It had always been my MO. Toxicity followed me, called to me, like a forbidden fruit to be craved.

My door silently opened. A sliver of light entered my room through the cracked door. The slight shift of energy caused me to peek my head out from under the comforter.

Little Friday stood in my bedroom's doorway. She carried her blankie. Her hand rested on the doorknob.

"I heard you ask for help," she whispered, her sweet child voice a contradiction to the anger and bile I spewed at myself, at my decisions.

"I did," was all I could say. I couldn't find a way to explain who and why, not to a child, not at this time of the morning.

"Mom and Auntie Shawna are not here," she said, removing her hand from the doorknob and taking a step into my room. "I checked Auntie's room. So I came to help."

"Do you normally sleep on your own?" I asked.

She shook her head.

I reached over to open the comforter closest to the door, and she crawled in. "What do you need help with?" she asked, eyeing me under the covers, able to see in the dark.

"Not feeling sad, I guess," I said, my truth in its most basic form.

She waited a moment, as if considering, and scooted to press her body to mine. She wrapped an arm over my abdomen. Her energy flowed over me in the gentlest way. "You're heavy," she assessed.

"I know." I almost cried but held it together for the sake of the innocent child. She didn't need to know the pains of the world yet.

"Why haven't you given your worries to the trees?" she asked, so innocently, as if she understood such adult worries. And maybe she did. I couldn't be sure what her abilities were, with her parents being two different kinds of Wild...and Hunter.

My mind blanked. This sweet, thoughtful, wise girl child was also Hunter.

I shifted in place. Friday kept her arm on me, adjusting its new spot.

"What's it like to have Hunter in you?" I asked earnestly. "What's it like to have Wild and Hunter?"

She thought for a moment. "Good."

I started to ask her a more pointed question, to get a more detailed answer, when she continued.

"I get to be strong, really strong, when I get older."

"Because of your Wild side?" I asked. Yes, Hunters were strong, but so were Wilds. And Wilds were better at using that strength to help and not hurt like the Hunters.

"My mama's people and my daddy's mama's people are powerful," she said.

I considered why a five-year-old would know enough to talk like this but then realized the world she lived in. I suspected she was taught early. As a young supernatural being living in a world of humans, her parents didn't have a choice.

I wondered if she never truly felt wholly huldra, or xana, or Hunter.

"But my daddy's dad's side is strong too," she said. She sighed. "I don't get to see them. None of Mama's people or Grandmama's people want to see the Hunter side of my family."

I hadn't thought about it this way, her having to cut off one side of her family, or what made her, her.

"Do they not let you know them?" I asked. "Your Hunter side?" I thought of another question before she answered my first. "How does that make you feel?"

She lay on her side, facing me. I couldn't see her features clearly under the covers, in the darkness, but my eyes had adjusted just enough to see her little smile and how she clutched at her blankie and pulled it closer to her face.

She smelled it. "It's for my own safety." She said the words as though she was repeating an adult's, which I assumed she was.

How she felt about it mattered more to me with the new information. I asked again, "How does that make you feel?" I wanted to add suggestions: Do you feel pulled in all directions? Do you feel like you don't belong anywhere? Do you feel at war inside, with three-quarters of you being Wild and a quarter Hunter? But I didn't want to risk putting feelings in her head she didn't already feel. So I waited.

"I feel like me," she finally said.

I contemplated her answer, fighting the urge to dismiss the simplicity of it.

"I'm not them," she added, helping me to understand. "I'm new. I'm me. I'm not a puzzle or a collage made up of others. I'm a new creation."

I lay there, beside a five-year-old with the wisdom of a fifty-five-year-old, mentally chewing on her explanation.

"I know what my grandpa did," she said. "I know that my great-grandpa did horrible things too. But I'm not them. I'm also not my grandmas. I'm me—only I get to decide." She paused to smooth a chubby hand across her blankie. "The trees tell me, everyone is handed a bowl of ingredients to bake their lives with. We don't get to choose the ingredients, but we do get to choose what we bake with them."

Her wisdom was not that of a fifty-five-year-old, but that of a five-hundred-and-five-year-old tree. She was most certainly a child of xana and huldra. The stories of how old huldra never died but rather become one with a tree when they reached a certain age seemed more real with each word Friday spoke.

"The plants were here first," I thought to say as I processed her words, "before any of our kinds, before the humans. They know best how to live a life of fulfillment within the energy of earth." It was a truth gifted to me in meditation, back before I decided to turn my whole life upside down.

A truth Friday reminded me of and cracked open for me, to reveal the deep, layered insides. I needed to receive wisdom from the trees.

"My tummy's growling," Friday said. "I'm hungry."

And just like that, the five-year-old returned, the little one demanding physical needs be met the moment they arose.

An idea popped into my head, a comfort food I hadn't made in a long while. Not since living in my new home with my new life. Suddenly, it felt like a comfort to be able to bake them again. "Do you like scones?" I asked.

She smiled and nodded.

"Let's make scones for when your mom and Shawna return," I suggested, lowering the thick comforter and sitting up in bed.

Friday sat up too and gathered her blankie into an easy-to-carry ball. "And Auntie Sarah," she added, excited. "Auntie Sarah loves scones more than anything!"

I only smiled as I helped her out of my bed and held her hand to the kitchen. I didn't answer, didn't tell her that no, Auntie Sarah was no longer allowed to step foot on my property. That I hoped I never had to see Auntie Sarah again.

CHAPTER SIXTEEN

Sarah

I needed to hurt something, kill something. Anger boiled in my blood and righteousness pushed it through my veins. But why? How?

I didn't have it in me to think, only to feel. And the way I felt...not even God himself would want to share the forest with me.

Small animals silenced their nighttime work. An owl perched on a branch, a safe distance away, watching me. I couldn't hunt them, didn't want to hunt them. I picked up a thick branch from the ground and snapped it in two.

"Fuck you!" I shouted to the woods, to myself for my need to destroy. I emotionally leaned in to that desire in search of...what? What did I need to destroy to feel better? Myself? Because I was pretty sure I already had back there. I'd pushed away the only real family I had left, Faline and Shawna, and outed myself as a Hunter and a liar to the one woman who both intrigued me and enticed me.

And this was how I repaid her. Pain and destruction.

Yup, seemed about right for my bloodline.

Marcus never told me his saint lived within him, that he could feel his saint attached to his Hunter, right under the surface, grasping for release. No one had told me that. Was it because I was a woman? Not supposed to feel such things? Not qualified to be the vessel of a saint?

Suddenly, I wished these things were true, that I wasn't qualified and couldn't possibly embody a saint, a holy person set on a single-minded control. I was an anomaly, a being that shouldn't exist.

I wished I didn't. Exist.

And maybe I wouldn't, at least not to anyone. I peered right and then left, behind me and in front. I didn't belong here. I didn't belong anywhere. I needed to run, to get away and find myself or lose myself. I couldn't be sure. But where? The trees would report my location back to the huldra, but they'd also know I needed to be alone, sort my crap out.

I started walking, the moon barely visible as it began to hide in the morning light. Clouds covered the sky, keeping the light spread thin. Fat water droplets fell from evergreen branches. Wet ferns brushed against my pants legs, leaving the gray sweats I wore darker and heavier below my knees.

Yes. I would stay in the woods awhile. Not Oriana's woods—no, I had to get away from these—but in the vast forest to the north. The rusalki and plenty others made the forests their homes, nature their grocery stores and places of worship. I could do the same.

A structure announced its presence in the distance, and as I neared, it came into focus. Oriana's yoga studio. Or at least, the beginnings of it—the bones of beams and a finished floor and roof. It only needed the walls and door installed. My trailer still stood beside the structure, a padlock hanging from the latch at the back of the trailer keeping the ramp door tightly enclosed.

Not a problem. I gripped the shackle of the padlock in my right hand and the body in my left. Tapping into my Hunter, I forced my hands in opposite directions and snapped the thing in two. I pulled open the double doors and released the ramp. A tiny overhead light automatically turned on when I opened the trailer up.

I may be a Hunter, but I refused to leave a job undone. Oriana deserved more than that, she deserved more than a Hunter too. But there was nothing I could do to fix that. Only, I could help her make her dreams come true, help her to be a yoga instructor.

At the moment, Oriana's yoga studio looked more like a summer pavilion than a year-round studio. But I had every intention of changing that. When she had discussed plans with Faline, she had made it crystal clear she didn't want the traditional cold-climate studio, complete with walls and electricity for warmth. No, she wanted it modeled after the warm-climate structures, appearing open and one with the surrounding nature.

I stood in the trailer and scanned its contents for something else crystal clear.

I locked in on the rolls of clear marine vinyl. Bingo. Not having to hang drywall would make finishing this project today a possibility. I only needed to install the door and affix the vinyl to the outer framing.

I had worked on this structure yesterday, and yet I felt a significant difference in my strength as I hauled two heavy rolls, each the length of a child, on my shoulders. My muscles and mind registered that they were of significant weight, but my body was able to carry and toss them onto the studio floor with ease.

First, the door, though. I walked back into the trailer and found the door quickly. The glass door, lined with wood at its edges, was Oriana's particular request. Faline had tried to discourage her from placing a glass door in the middle of the woods in western Washington. Our winters caused great evergreens to fall and their branches to snap up in the wind and plow through whatever nature deemed destructible. But Oriana wouldn't budge.

I lifted the door over my head with ease and carried it that way, as though the top of my head was its resting place.

Leave it to Oriana to choose glass in the woods. She had told Faline she'd have a discussion with the trees and beings in her woods, and if they still deemed her structure breakable, then she would respect their wishes. Even Faline, communicator with trees, whose foremothers were literally parts of the oldest trees on the earth, thought Oriana's response odd. But then again, Faline didn't talk to forest beings.

That's because Oriana is special, I caught myself thinking.

This yoga studio was her freedom, her next step to the life of her dreams.

I smiled, proud of myself. This would be the perfect parting gift.

Not that I wanted to part, but I had gotten a sneak peek into the witch's personality in the little time we'd known one another, and she wasn't the type to change her mind when she was done with someone.

She was definitely done with me once she saw I was a Hunter.

I didn't want to ask myself how I felt about that, the way I had tried to start asking myself whenever something out of the ordinary presented itself.

I didn't want to know the answer, didn't want to delve into the pit that was my hurt. I just needed to get this last thing done, and I would figure everything out later.

Rejected. I felt rejected.

Oof. My heart squeezed in pain.

I'd told myself I wouldn't ask.

I placed the door gently onto the floor of pretreated lumber and stood to inhale a mouthful of fresh morning air.

Growing up female in a man's world came with the added bonus of continual rejection. I never fit my family's idea of a good Hunter woman—or, should I say, a Hunter's future wife.

I had too many thoughts, too many questions. I needed concepts to make sense before I could completely accept them, and when you're a woman in a man's world, no one has the patience or time to explain anything that doesn't directly pertain to your purpose in life, to make baby boy Hunters.

Girls were loved, but not respected. We had been loved as vessels, whereas the boys had been loved as living beings.

I turned to head back to the trailer, to grab the drill, drill bit, and hanging fixtures for the door. Yeah, maybe I should have been used to rejection, but I still didn't like it and certainly didn't want to stay and continue to experience it.

I really didn't need the reminder that I wasn't wanted. I scolded myself for staying after Oriana kicked the ex-Hunter males out. I should have left with my brothers.

Another thought occurred to me. Yeah, Marcus and my other ex-Hunter brothers had left the establishment and renounced what our forefathers stood for, but did their Hunters still live? They had to. So then, weren't they *still* Hunters?

No. I shook my head as I hung the door with ease and screwed the hinge plates into the doorframe.

I laughed. "Now I'm talking to myself," I said, still talking to myself.

It was ridiculous, how this witch had my head spinning and my heart doubting.

With the glass door perfectly in place—I swung it open and shut a few times to test its positioning—I moved to the clear vinyl. I rolled what would be the faux wall-length windows out onto the studio floor and absently patted my tool belt for my measuring tape.

When my hand found nothing resembling a tool belt, I looked down, and sure enough, I wasn't wearing one. I shook my head and stood to tromp back through the rain to my trailer. I scanned what was left of the contents: a toolbox, leftover boards, leftover boxes of nails, rolls of vinyl, but no tool belt.

I threw my hands up. "Crap, of course it has to be in my truck." Which was in front of Oriana's home.

I caught myself sulking—I wouldn't be able to finish this for Oriana before I left—but emotionally pulled it together.

I didn't need to measure and cut the vinyl for ease of installation. I could simply hoist the vinyl up and start stapling it to the wooden framing. Humans need a device to warm the vinyl enough that it would stretch easily, and the vinyl had to be measured precisely before it was stretched. And when I had worked with this clear vinyl material before, I had followed the same protocol as humans. Like humans, I wasn't strong enough to carry the roll and stretch it myself.

But now, that wasn't the case.

I laughed sarcastically to myself and walked back to the yoga studio. I could manage just fine without my tool belt.

Halfway between the trailer and the studio, a strong breeze joined the rain, now moving sideways.

Okay, not gonna make this easier on me, huh?

"Hunter…" I heard, trailing on the wind. The word whispered through the trees as though they too were judging me and insisting I leave.

I looked around, peered out at the evergreens, feathers of emerald soaked and dripping. Nothing. My Hunter roused from her rest. My eyes shut to better access my unseen surroundings as though it was a common practice.

Except I'd never done it before.

It was as though my Hunter knew how to access parts of me and will those parts to comply.

Something felt off, but I couldn't pinpoint what that was. Some sort of energy, faint and almost nonexistent, but not carrying Oriana's energy signature, and definitely not invited.

How did I know it wasn't invited, though?

That one fact roused my Hunter even more. Only, where I felt confusion, she brought comfort, as though she placed a weighted blanket of confidence and knowing over the exposed and fearful parts of my being to calm the anxiety. It worked too.

I stood out in the drizzle for a moment longer before brushing off the voice in the breeze and continuing on with my task. I wanted it done so I could be gone by morning's full light.

I tossed the roll of vinyl onto my shoulder and slid the box cutter— all I could find in the trailer to cut with—into the front pocket of my sweats. Its weight dragged the fabric low around my hips as I worked.

Crap, the staple gun.

With the roll on my shoulder, I walked back to the trailer with ease and riffled through a rubber toolbox bungee-corded to the hooks on the floor of the trailer to stay in place when in motion. I slipped the handle of the staple gun onto the collar of my T-shirt and headed back to the structure.

"Hunter…" the wind proclaimed again.

Or was it goading me?

Did wind goad?

My Hunter insisted I toss everything I held and search the woods for a threat, but I held strong and refused. Oriana deserved a finished yoga studio. She deserved to have her dreams come true. She had lived through too much to get this far and have to wait even longer for the future she yearned for.

I started at the middle back of the structure and raised the roll upright, stapling vinyl to the outer framing. Once the roll was secured, I pulled it taut, but not enough to release it from its staples or pull down the board altogether, which I had no doubt my Hunter was capable of. I stapled the clear sheet to the next board, and continued on.

A breeze ruffled my hair, and I wished I had thought to wear a beanie.

"Hear me," a voice said on the wind, only louder than the wind this time, "Hunter…"

I shook my head, feeling silly for responding to the wind, but also resolute in my task.

"I have to finish this," I heard myself say. A flood of desire to touch Oriana, to sit with her, to take in the lavender and patchouli scent of her soft skin, to hear her laugh, her voice.

I pushed on.

Oriana had trusted me. She let her guard down for me and bared her soul, even if only a small piece, to see how I would handle it. And in response to her gift, I pretended to be someone she could trust. Yeah, that made me a liar, but didn't it also make me a fraud? A manipulator like the others she had been with? How was I any different?

I thought of her ex, Steven, the way he stood in her driveway and demanded of her. I wasn't like him. I wouldn't take from her and then when it was my turn to give, take some more while calling her selfish for wanting to be on the receiving end. No, I might have taken her trust and vulnerability, but I refused to give her nothing in return.

"You forget yourself, Hunter," the voice said again, eerily closer than before. The hairs on the back of my neck stood, but I pressed on, stapling vinyl to wood.

"I won't leave," I told the disembodied voice.

I had allowed fear to hide my truth from Oriana. I wasn't going to let it keep me from giving her her dream studio before I exited her life for good.

Three more framing posts to staple the vinyl to. Then I would leave.

A mist rolled in, like the kind that settled on trees before the sun rose in the early fall and winter mornings. Only this mist didn't rest atop trees, didn't tangle in the evergreens' needles. This mist hovered over the leaf-covered ground, the size of a human being. I watched it continue to form itself, swirls cascading into one another, making the mist thicker, denser.

I kept an eye on it out of the corner of my vision and moved quicker. Three more, I told myself.

I pressed the staple gun into the last outer wooden beam and pulled the box cutter from my pocket, swiftly cutting the stapled vinyl from the roll.

The mist, now opaque as white frosted glass and four times as thick, slowly made its way toward me and the studio. Let it study the building all it wanted. I was not planning to stick around for the tour.

I only needed to get the rest of the vinyl roll into the trailer, along with the staple gun and box cutter, close up the back end, and be on my way. The keys to my truck were on Oriana's entry table, for Faline. I wasn't planning on taking anything with me, other than what I already wore.

Halfway to the trailer, something tapped me on my upper back. I spun, out of habit, right into the body of mist.

I backed up, shocked and unsure if walking into spirit mist was a bad mistake. I tried to brush the wispy vines from my face. Each time mist touched my bare skin, warm tingles accompanied it.

"Hear me!" the voice commanded.

I released the tools and supplies I held, as though my hands had minds of their own. The gear dropped into the mud, splashing droplets on my sweats. I tried to run, but my legs refused to budge. I panicked, and my Hunter responded.

Without thinking, I crouched, my knees bending enough to keep my balance lower to the ground, to keep me upright if the spirit tried to shove me.

I assumed it was a spirit, but it could have been anything. A witch worked within these woods.

The newly formed cross tattoo on my forearm burned. I tried to rub it, move the blood around in my arm, but my hands refused to budge.

I couldn't move. I was frozen.

Fear soured my mouth and tightened my muscles.

The mist gathered itself, growing increasingly dense and taking the shape of a woman, short in stature. The mist had no color, but it wore a dress. Tiny water droplets continually rearranged themselves within the mist, sparkling and blinking whenever they caught the light of the moon. The hem of the dress hovered over the leaf-littered ground, shifting as a skirt would with each breeze.

"The forest has called you to this place," the voice now said, fully woman and fully present. A petite face barely made itself known through the mist, brow, nose and lips beneath a thin veil of shifting fabric.

Who are you? I could only think, not speak, because my lips were now frozen in place as well.

"I am she who was here first," the woman answered. "My sisters and I protect and govern the waterfall here, Obsidian Falls."

There were other groups of women, not Wild nor witch, who existed and protected?

"Go back to your love," she instructed.

If I could have shaken my head, I would have.

I couldn't stay. Oriana didn't want me as a Hunter, and I couldn't exactly change that part about me. I would forever be in limbo between the world of Hunters and the world of supernaturals, never fully belonging to either. At least Marcus had Wild blood in him. I didn't. I was fully Hunter, and there was nothing I could do about it.

"You, Sarah Johns, are no mere Huntress." The woman's face defined itself, until eyes shone of light and darkness, the mist swirling around sockets. Long, straight hair floated around her head like she was in water.

I had never heard the term *Huntress* used except as a slur, to refer to evil women, usually Wild Women, hunting poor, vulnerable human men.

The mist neared me in a swift breath and caught me up, blanketing me in a freezing embrace.

Warm tingles covered my body while my core froze. I couldn't move. Couldn't scream for help.

"Rise, Brigid!" the mist woman proclaimed. "Rise!"

My body vibrated. The intense pain of new tattoos etching themselves into my skin suffused my body.

This is how I die, I thought as shadows encased me, blanketing my vision. All sense of being drained from me. My pumping blood ceased, freezing in my veins.

Then, everything went dark.

CHAPTER SEVENTEEN

Oriana

My new red coffeepot beeped to let me know it had finished brewing the full pot I'd put on. Still in my robe, I shuffled to pour a cup, added creamer, and headed back to the couch.

Friday picked her head up to return to lying on my lap, as she had done before the coffeepot beckoned me.

I placed my full mug on the side table and adjusted Friday's blanket, and she repositioned her head on my lap.

My right hand held the steaming hot mug to my lips while my left hand stroked Friday's fine, wavy brown hair in the soft light of one lit lamp in the living room.

The rest of the house was dark. Scones baked in the oven, filling the home with the warm comforting sweetness of cold-weather treats.

My phone buzzed, and before giving it any thought, my hand shot to check the screen, hoping it was a text from Sarah.

My heart sank. No, just a spam solicitor email. I put the phone back on the side table. Sarah didn't have my number.

Good. Then she couldn't text constantly trying to persuade me to look past her lies and…and…Well, there wasn't much else I could say against her.

She was a Hunter. Wasn't that enough?

Faline quietly entered through my front door, as though she was slinking into a house full of sleeping people. Not this morning. No one slept this morning. Shawna wasn't too far behind. She shut the door, and the two Wild Women stood in my small entryway, assessing my face.

"I'm not mad at you," I half groaned, half whined. "I'm pissed at Sarah for lying."

Faline and Shawna sat on the love seat opposite my couch, its back to the great living room window. They looked spent, emotionally and physically.

"It was not our intent to deceive you," Shawna started.

"I know," I said. But I didn't. Why, in my mind, had I assumed these two didn't realize Sarah was a Hunter? Wishful thinking, possibly. Probably.

A new cut of betrayal formed along my heart, invisible to all but me. It would create, in time, a new scar I'd have to live with, combat, and eventually overcome.

I was so tired of overcoming.

I thought to kick them out right then and there. I was done with this whole mess. My yoga studio wasn't worth this. My dreams could be achieved some other way. Yeah, it would take more time and effort, but at least building a new life that way wouldn't include my heart being broken into a million pieces.

But if they left, Friday would leave too. And she didn't deserve to be rushed out of here in the early morning hours. Not without her promised scones.

I allowed myself that one concession. I would wait until the scones were done.

My hand had absently paused stroking Friday's hair, and she reached a little hand up to tap my fingers awake. I gave a small smile and resumed.

When I kept silent, only allowing the hint of my smile to show, Shawna spoke again, as though the tension made her uncomfortable. "We had allotted a certain amount of time to get the studio done. When you turned away the Hunter males, it extended our build time. If we let Sarah leave with her brothers, it would have put us over. We have lives and commitments to get back to." Her eyes were big and honest and caring.

Too little, too late.

"Well, then," I said, taking a sip of coffee to seem like I wasn't shaking inside. "I think today's as good as any for you two to get back to your lives."

Faline shot me a look. Her eyes hardened. "Are you kicking us out?"

"No," I said, the hint of defensiveness in my voice exposing the reason behind the decision. "I am saying you've fulfilled your services, and hopefully I have too."

Faline leaned forward. She balled her fists at her sides. I could tell she was trying to refrain from giving me a piece of her mind. "How do you know you've completed your training of Friday?"

I would miss Friday, that was true. But I also had to stick to my personal boundaries. I sucked at that, and there was no time like the present to work on it.

"As much as you've finished on the yoga studio, I've finished helping Friday." I wasn't sure how accurate that statement was, but it was all I could think to say.

Because I didn't want Friday to feel like a pawn in all this, or unwanted by me, I added, "Whatever is left that she needs from me can be done over the internet, video calls and stuff."

Friday smiled. And at first I figured it was the idea of seeing me again. But then she spoke. "It's okay, Mama, I am done learning from the trees here."

We all looked to the little girl, who peacefully rested in a space full of tension.

"You were to learn from Ms. Oriana, honey," Faline said.

"Not really," Friday answered as though they were disagreeing on something as unimportant as a hue of color. "The trees of her forest introduced me to the original coven of this place. Their tree wisdom is different than ours."

"My coven ancestors connected with you?" I asked the little girl with awe.

She gave a silent nod.

Before Cedarsprings was a town in the mountains of western Washington, it existed as an uninhabitable area full of mountains, treacherous cliffs, and otherworldly beings, both coming from and drawn to the great waterfall hidden deep within the forest on the hill.

Back in the Old West, a group of women, of witches, found each other, brothel prostitutes tired of trying to exist within the confines of patriarchy.

Witches could not safely practice in those days without being ostracized at best and burned at worst. Witch killings weren't prevalent in the 1800s, but they still happened. The townsmen would gather under the secrecy of night, claiming righteousness, justifying their cruel acts. They would lock a witch in her home, along with whatever family she had with her, and light her home on fire.

History books failed to speak of this, of course. The righteous men had made it look like local tribes of Native Americans had been the culprits, burning the cabins of their friends.

So these witches picked up and left, from all across the United States. They say they followed a call to go west, and so they did. They all wound up at the bottom of the great waterfall, until their coven was complete.

Together, their power had been strong enough to bind the portal within the waterfall, to restrict its access from those who traveled to this world to do harm. They became the saviors and protectors of Obsidian Falls, naming the waterfall after the stone best known for protection against dark forces.

"What did they teach you?" I couldn't help but ask Friday, of my heroic foremothers.

Only in coven rituals have I experienced more than one of my coven ancestors at a time. I had the spirit of one hanging around my house every now and again, the witch spirit who insisted on kicking out the Hunters. But that was all.

Before Friday could answer, I followed up with another thought. "They hate Hunters." I didn't have to finish the thought audibly. We all already knew what that meant.

Faline sat up straighter, the look of a protective mother ready to pounce, Wild or human was the same. Set jaw. Steel eyes cautioning to tread lightly. Shawna pressed her palm to Faline's thigh, which seemed to make no difference at all to the Wild mother of a part-Hunter child.

"No." I backpedaled. At this point, I could give two shits if Faline was pissed at me or not. She could leave for all I cared, and never come back. But Friday was who I considered when I tried to explain myself. I didn't want to never see her again.

"I'm only saying I'm shocked that they would work with Friday because she's part Hunter, and the coven, especially the original coven, has a strong hatred for Hunters. It's the reason I kicked your Hunters off my property in the first place. A foremother told me to."

"Cadence?" Friday asked, her little head tilted up, looking at me with innocent questioning eyes.

I couldn't help but smile in response.

"I don't know her name," I explained. My coven sisters had assured me it took time before the foremothers revealed their names to new coven members. "But she likes to hang around my place and doesn't tend to mince words."

Friday's smile stayed put as she rested her head back down. "Yeah, that's Cadence. Alice and Gertrude are much nicer, but Cadence is pretty nice when no one is around."

I'd heard the names of our foremothers spoken in rituals, but none had introduced themselves to me, not yet. But they had to a little girl with Hunter blood in her veins? How did that make any sense at all?

"What's going on here?" Faline said, no longer able to sit in place. She shot up to stand, and I nearly jumped in shock at her quick movement.

Surely a Wild wouldn't hurt a witch, especially not a witch who had a resting Wild offspring on her lap.

"I was told to come here. It's not like I wanted to leave my home." Faline's hands rested on her hips. "And then my husband and his brothers were sent away, leaving me to trust you to guide my child without my watching over her, so I could build the structure you asked for. You forced me into this spot, and now…now, this?"

She waved her hands out in front of her.

"Friday, get your things," she said, staring at her daughter until the little girl rose from my lap and stood.

"Mama," Friday said, "it's not Ms. Oriana's fault. This was the plan, why we came."

We all froze and stared at the little girl.

"This trip wasn't just for me," the little girl went on, such adult words on such a small voice. "The spirits never do a thing for only one reason. Their work is for all of us."

"What does that mean, it wasn't just for you?" I asked and waited on bated breath with the other women in the room.

Suddenly the energy in the space changed from angry tension to unknown fear. I preferred the former over the latter. Chills ran along my spine as though a spirit had entered the room, but I felt none around.

"I came for you," Friday said to me, her round cheeks rosy. "It was okay that you ran the boys off, because they weren't in the plan. Only Sarah was."

My heart sank. "Sarah was a part of the plan? What plan?"

Friday inhaled deeply and exhaled before answering. "Ostara is coming," she said. "It's nearly here, actually."

Ostara, the Sabbat of new beginnings, our celebration of spring and new life. I grabbed my phone from the side table to look at the date. Sure as shit, tonight was my Ostara Sabbat ritual with my coven sisters. Why hadn't Serene mentioned it earlier when we were texting? How had I forgotten?

I placed my phone back down and stared at the little girl, speechless. We all did.

Huge evergreens loomed outside the windows, their branches dancing in the uptick of wind.

"It's okay," she said, now walking down the hall to the room where she and her mom had stayed. I suspected she was obeying her mother and grabbing her things to go. "We're done here. Auntie Sarah's Hunter is free."

Tears formed behind my eyes. "What does that mean?" I asked. "Her Hunter is free?"

Friday didn't turn to acknowledge my confusion or answer my question. Three grown women stood, silent, in the shadowy living room, waiting for the little one to emerge from the guest room to share more insight.

Was Sarah fully Hunter now? Had my kicking her out caused her to turn away from the Wild Woman way and return to her roots? Did I now have a fully formed Hunter on my property? Had I just unleashed a witch killer...on the same property as Obsidian Falls? The waterfall my coven was charged to protect from supernaturals who wished to do harm?

A hard knock sounded at my front door, jolting us out of the current moment and into another. We stared at the door.

I hesitantly made my way over and opened it.

A gust of cold air swept in from behind a police officer. His squad car sat running in my makeshift driveway, another officer watching us all from the passenger's seat.

"Oriana Ravenswood?" the officer said, his graying facial scruff a week past a good trim. His uniform looked as though he was at the end of a shift, rumpled and unkempt. The man appeared exhausted, from his red eyes to his hunched back.

"That's me," I said. "How can I help you?"

"We received a rather distressed call," he answered.

"I didn't call," I responded. I looked behind me to see if either of the Wild Women had called the police.

"When was the last time you saw your husband, Steven?" he asked, shifting his weight from one foot to another.

"Ex-husband," I corrected. "The papers have already been filed."

He gave a nod and continued, "He called us, from here on your land. Something about a red monster coming after him."

I tilted my head in confusion. "A red monster?"

The officer looked as though he was going to smirk but quickly straightened his face. "Is he known to participate in drug use?"

I shook my head. "Is he okay?"

The officer shrugged. "We found his car at the bottom of the hill, beginning of your driveway. His phone is broken, smashed, sitting on the driver's seat. Doors are locked."

That was very odd.

I thought of the beings in my woods. None could be seen as a red monster. Whatever that meant. Unless it had come through the portal. Beings could travel here from other realms, like the Underworld, if they were able to use the right energy signature to locate our portal.

The officer interrupted my thoughts. "Do we have your permission to have a search team out here this afternoon? If we can't locate him by then?"

"Yes," I said. "Of course. Whatever I can do to help."

He gave a thankful nod and turned to walk down my porch steps. Back still turned, he half waved before lowering himself into the squad car. He shut the door. As though it was an afterthought, he rolled down the passenger side window and said, "I'm sure there's nothing to worry about. He sounded like he was on something, which would make sense with the crushed phone. He probably locked himself out of his car. I bet we'll find him somewhere out here, sleeping it off. Thankfully, the temperatures aren't freezing."

Without a response from me, he rolled up the passenger window and the two cops drove off down my driveway.

I shut the door and turned to Shawna and Faline. "Did you see Steven out there?"

"We watched from a distance, made sure he made it to his little truck at the bottom of your hill," Shawna said. "But then we came back. Figured he'd gotten into his car, so he was leaving."

"Sarah," was all I said. "I saw the way she looked at him from the porch, like she wanted to off him."

Faline shook her head. "No, she wouldn't. And she's not red. He said it was a red monster."

I scoffed. How could she be so sure it wasn't Sarah? I headed to my room to grab the jeans and sweater crumpled on my bedroom floor.

"The old Hunter blades had a red stone," I reminded from my room. "Red stones have kinda always been their thing." I threw my robe and pajamas onto my bed and pulled on my dirty clothes.

"But Sarah doesn't have a Hunter's blade," Faline countered, standing outside my open bedroom door. "She's female. They never gave her one."

"There is no red monster in my woods," I spat in defense.

Sarah was supernatural. Something about her could have looked red. Her eyes maybe. Maybe she carried a red weapon they didn't know about.

"And she's the only one on my property with the ability and reason and temper to be seen as a monster," I added, exiting my room past Faline.

Faline and Shawna refused to budge in their defense of the female Hunter.

"Just because she's a Hunter doesn't make her a killer," Faline argued, turning to face me as I moved around my house.

I caught the defensiveness in her voice.

I stopped, my black cloak across my forearm. "Faline," I said, this time more concrete in my opinion of Sarah than ever before, "your husband is only half Hunter, and who knows how his Wild Woman side tempers and changes his Hunter abilities. Sarah's not half. She's full.

She has nothing to temper herself and no formal training on controlling her Hunter. You cannot sit here and definitively tell me it wasn't her."

The oven timer blared, screeching that the scones were done. The three of us jumped with nerves.

Only, when I landed back on solid footing, I didn't stay put. I bolted through the kitchen, past Friday, Faline, and Shawna, and out the back door.

I had a waterfall to protect.

I had a Hunter to find.

CHAPTER EIGHTEEN

Sarah

Everything was dark, and loud, and...wet?

Something hard and chiseled poked into my back. Moist air drenched me and droplets wound down my face. I wiped at my eyes before attempting to open them. The scent of fresh water with traces of mud and the sweetness of decaying plants swirled on a strong breeze that didn't ebb and flow but kept pushing in on me.

I blinked. Tiny droplets clung to my eyelashes, giving the world a blurry affect. I pushed my weight from the rock with my left arm. A dull muscle ache and skin tenderness announced the presence of a new tattoo. I sat up to examine my forearm. While a conventional Hunter cross now lived on my right forearm, a different type of cross lived on the left side. Only, the beams on this cross were equal in length, forming what looked more like four spokes of a wheel than the blade and hilt of a Hunter's dagger, designed after the cross.

Stronger than the roar of the waterfall I lay behind, a new remembrance of what had just happened shot into my chest.

I sat up and doubled over, my stomach empty and twisting. She was mine and I had let her go.

Mine.

Shocked, I checked myself. No one person belonged to anyone. Oriana owed me nothing. She had made it clear she didn't want Hunters on her land. There was nothing I could do about that.

Still, the...the knowing that she was mine dug into me, penetrated my muscles, down into my cells. Lived in the marrow of my bones.

I would never be myself without her.

No, no, that was seriously not healthy. Hunter marriages were the pinnacle of toxic, so I knew which flags were red, and if someone had said what I was thinking, it would be red flag city.

But what I felt didn't feel toxic. It felt fulfilling, strengthening. Like pieces of a 3-D puzzle that are perfect on their own, but build a stronger structure of support together. As though something inside knew this to be true, beyond a shadow of a doubt.

"That's just the love cocktail of chemicals pulsing through my brain," I responded to myself, loud enough to hear my voice over the water.

My arm pulsed in pain, and I looked down at the tattoos. The equal cross on my left and a Hunter cross on my right. I didn't know the meaning of the equal cross, but I already preferred it.

"Good, you have awoken finally."

I jumped up to stand, nearly slipping on slick stone in the process, but saw no one with me in the cave behind the waterfall.

Mist, like an arrow, shot through the curtain of water and into the cavern, quickly taking the shape of a woman whose dress hovered over the wet stone.

The spirit in the woods.

"How do you feel?" Her words were softer than earlier.

She showed no distinct facial characteristics but had the shadowed lines of a face. The mist, in the form of a woman with a dress on, remained in place, despite the ever-moving air, pushed by the movement of roaring water.

How did I feel?

I wanted to scream in physical pain, but mostly heartache. I wanted to beat the slick rock till my knuckles bled. I wanted to run.

"I feel like I need to go," I finally answered.

"You will not run away," she said.

"Away from what?" I shot back. "Away from a witch who told me to leave?"

"Away from yourself."

I exhaled as if she'd punched me in the gut. She might as well have.

"Don't worry," I heard myself say with the unbridled honesty I revealed to no one. "I know I'll never be able to outrun myself."

"Her fire is power and your fire is life, and together you two will set the world ablaze with the power of life," the spirit said, her words barely audible, conjuring up an old sense of knowing. Her words bloomed within me as truth the moment they were spoken. "You were chosen by St. Brigid. If any a woman was worthy of my Oriana, it is you."

"*Your* Oriana?" I asked.

"She is a great coven daughter, one of our own. She has flourished as of late, leaning on her own understanding, learning to trust herself. Trust builds confidence which builds the strength of a witch's ability to manifest. Her focus becomes more acute as she releases the opinions of others and walks by her own torch." The words came with no pause, one on top of the other. "Oriana has manifested you. She has called to you."

Before I could argue, which I was going to, the spirit continued, "You have answered her call, heard and knew her voice. From the moment you saw her, your knowing was made known to you. If you were not ready, not able to also trust your own self, you would not have answered the call."

If she wouldn't let me argue, I was going to avoid the topic altogether. "What do you mean St. Brigid chose me?" I asked. Male Hunters were named after popes and saints, and it didn't mean that saints actually occupied their bodies. Though, according to Faline, they did offer assistance.

The mist shifted closer to me. I jumped back at its movement and then straightened myself. When it neared a second time, I held steady. It wisped and floated into the shape of a woman again.

"The saints have been known to occupy the bodies of Hunters." She moved closer still, the form of a woman not dissipating in the slightest. "Women as well."

So Faline wasn't wrong.

I thought back to my childhood, of the great Hunters taught to us in Sunday school and in our homeschooled history courses, the Hunters who stood out from the rest as exemplarily, the heroes we were to model our own lives after. Well, the boys.

Technically, I was to model my behavior after docile, submissive women of the Bible, particularly one of the women who was so humble she was nameless and was only referred to by the book of the Bible she's found in. That's how godly she was—she'd given up all sense of self, even her name. If there had been heroic female Hunters, they weren't spoken of, not even in our history.

"St. Brigid," the spirit said into my mind, "has a secret, though." Layers of laughter filled my mind, and I fought the urge to cover my ears. "She has been wearing the cloak of another. The priests could not convert the followers of Brigid, Goddess of the flame at hearth, temple, and forge. She who inspires. As long as her people followed, she refused to leave them. She allowed the priests to twist her purpose and her stories and call her a saint. Now she has decided to come again for her people, through you."

"So she's the one I've been feeling? Not my Hunter?" I didn't know why this hit me so painfully, to not be a Hunter. To be merely a Hunter's daughter again, allowed on the outskirts of the group, but never holding a place in the middle. Maybe that was why Oriana had trusted me. The witch hadn't sensed a Hunter.

A spark of hope lit in my chest. If I wasn't a true Hunter, and it was an ancient Goddess moving through me, Oriana would want to be with me.

"The Goddess Brigid had access to you through your Hunter," the spirit answered audibly, as if she knew my thoughts were a mess she couldn't wade through.

Once she had my attention, she spoke into my mind. "She is a saint, and your creators made sure only saints and popes had access to Hunters. It was their way of ensuring other beings couldn't infiltrate their ranks, and it enables them to claim they are near divinity as vessels."

To say I failed to wrap my head around the spirit's words would be a gross understatement. "Wait," I said, water rushing all around us. "Are you telling me it's not a pope or a saint who's been trying to take over? It's actually been a Goddess?"

CHAPTER NINETEEN

Oriana

I contemplated issuing a call to arms to my coven sisters but decided not to call and wake them early on a weekday morning. Sarah was my problem to fix. I had invited a Hunter onto my property. I had—

No, I wouldn't admit I had fallen for a Hunter. I wanted to shake that realization off with the raindrops on my cloak and in my hair.

Nah, the raindrops belonged.

The Hunter didn't.

I trudged through my woods, toward the Obsidian Falls waterfall. Of course the Hunter would be attracted to the forbidden interdimensional portal, the existence of which only coven sisters knew. A secret we each took an oath we'd die protecting. The reason this was my property.

I wondered how the Hunter woman knew. Did she torture it out of a coven sister? Did a fellow witch spill the truth behind the waterfall's use moments before taking her last breath?

Fear hit me in the gut when I considered the possibility that a coven sister could have received a warning on my behalf, from an ancestor, and came to check things out. What if she had unknowingly found Sarah instead of me? What if Sarah forced the secret of the waterfall's importance out of her?

Hunters were soulless beings who claimed to protect against the soulless. It was a nasty facade they had upheld for far too long. Served them right the Wild Women had brought their reign to ruins and fire.

No, someone would have called me by now if that was the case. Supernatural baddies couldn't just hang out around here without us knowing. No one from my coven mentioned getting a feeling or even a warning.

What was I going to walk into? My mind whirred with possibilities.

My thick, black cloak over my black hoodie kept me hidden in the dark. My athame was set securely in my leather holster at my hip. My black all-weather boots reached my upper jeans-covered calf and protected my legs from the elements and any plants that might grab at my flesh. My hair, released from its ponytail, wildly danced upon the wind, absorbing its energy and siphoning it into my own.

Morning light filtered through thick gray clouds, causing the hues of green leaves and pine needles to pop with color.

The properties of my coven sisters all connected, converging at Obsidian Falls. Last year, when I had pulled into Cedarsprings with all I owned in a rental moving truck and a little commuter car pulled behind, this is what I came for. This land. An Obsidian Falls coven daughter returning to the place of her foremothers, to continue what they had started.

Only, I hadn't assumed, at the time, that I would end up having to protect the falls against a lover, or someone I had thought was a lover. Sounded about right for me and my inability to pick a suitable partner.

My half-finished yoga studio stood in the distance, a white trailer beside it. I tromped toward it. My dream wouldn't be completed with joy and celebration. I would now be completing the build alone and angry.

This was a problem I had created, so it was going to have to be a problem I fixed.

But when I neared the structure, I noticed the door I'd picked out online. It hung securely in place, all glass and gorgeousness. On its lintel hung an ornament of some kind. I picked up my pace to see what adorned my studio, if it was an omen set there by the beings of the woods. I stood on the top step to enter my finished yoga studio. It was beautiful, enclosed in clear vinyl to keep the feel of being outside, like I'd requested.

It was gorgeous, everything I had imagined.

My heart jumped for joy. I could start yoga classes. My dreams were coming true.

Reality broke through my moment of fantasy. I reached to remove the thing hanging from a nail in the center of the lintel. It seemed the only purpose of the nail was to hang this ornament. I turned it over in my hands. Made of twigs, it was Brigid's cross.

What was Brigid's cross doing hanging from my yoga studio? Brigid had never been a deity I worked with. I preferred Goddesses less entwined in the church. To me, even her cross was still a cross.

I turned the arranged twigs and inspected the craftmanship. Thicker twigs made the base of the structure, while smaller, thinner twigs wound around the thicker ones. I'd only ever seen this type of symbol done in wheat stalks and other more pliable supplies from nature. To create this, from difficult to mold wood, took skill.

I reached up to place the thing back on the nail, to hang above my yoga studio door. Despite my dislike of cross symbols, it would be foolish to remove it until I figured out where it came from.

For all I knew, this was a gift from the Goddess herself.

The temptation to linger kept me in place. Standing on tiptoe to rehang Brigid's cross, I peeked through the glass of the studio's front door.

So badly, I wanted to open the door before me and sit in the middle of the studio floor. I imagined the space filled with people meditating, stretching, connecting their hearts to their minds and learning to flow naturally with both. This was a space of healing, and just being near it made my athame seem unnecessary for bloodshed and very necessary for slicing fruit to set out in appreciation to the unseen beings of the forest. For ritual rather than death of evil.

I imagined Sarah.

And before I could get to the part of my fantasy where we give thanks to the woods together, tears sprang to my eyes. My chest ached and tightened.

I wished my coven ancestors would guide me, show me what to do. But none hovered nearby. None came to my call. Not even the trees were speaking to me tonight—or should I say this morning.

I knew why they were all silent in my woods, when only days ago they had been present and watchful. A Hunter was in their midst. A supernatural being set on control, whether they wanted to be or not.

Whether Sarah wanted to oppress or not, it was in her, some part of her she would never be able to fully fight or deny. And it was only a matter of time before her trickle of Hunter domination and control would turn into a waterfall. It was in her nature. She couldn't help herself.

When I had originally placed a protection spell over my property and the surrounding woods, I had made it clear that only those who were here for the coven's best and highest good were allowed. All others were not. A Hunter was clearly not walking the earth for the best and highest good of others outside their organization, even if their organization no longer existed.

The beings in my woods protected me. But I protected them too.

If my ex had seen a red monster, how well was I protecting my forest? The beings in my forest? I had invited a loose cannon of a Hunter onto my property, and who knew what damage she had already caused.

I released the twig symbol of Brigid onto its nail and jumped from the top step onto the ground. I needed to wipe the Sarah fantasies from my mind. She was not my future. She could not add to my life, only take away from it. I had a habit for falling for people like this, people who were bad for me, people who hurt others and would eventually turn their selfishness upon me. Nobody else deserved to pay the price for that, outside of me. Not in my woods.

My boots hit the ground at a run.

CHAPTER TWENTY

Sarah

I was behind a waterfall. An old Obsidian Falls coven member's spirit, the hem of her mist-formed dress hovering over the wet stone, was speaking to me.

And…and I had a Goddess inside me.

What kind of *Twilight Zone* crap was this?

"You were brought to this place," the spirit said, speaking into my mind, "to ensure Brigid's arrival."

I started to pace the small space behind the rushing blanket of water but nearly slipped on the slick stone with each step. I yanked off my boots and peeled down my socks, my bare toes offering more grip and traction.

"To this waterfall?" I asked out loud as though I was just talking to a friend, while setting my boots aside and realizing there was no dry spot to put them. Not that they weren't already drenched.

"To the Obsidian Falls coven's domain," the spirit responded. "For generations we have been keeping the area safe, keeping the waterfall's portal from allowing unloving beings to pass through to this side."

My chest squeezed at the mention of unloving beings. Was I not one of those beings? I was a Hunter. The coven hated me, and rightly so. My forefathers nearly obliterated their foremothers during the Inquisitions and Witch Hunts. Wasn't it only right that I be drawn to this location to be killed, to rid the world of one more unloving being?

A new fear slithered into my thoughts. What if the Hunters

originally came through a portal? What if they were truly among the evil that entered this land?

"To be Hunter-born is not the same as born into evil," the witch spirit said aloud, her voice now booming above the rushing water. She transformed into a pillar of mist, the bottom inches away from the stone floor, the top also inches away from the stone ceiling.

A push, gentle and guiding, came from nowhere and backed me into the farthest rocky wall from the ledge of the waterfall.

"This land is your chrysalis," the spirit whispered into my mind.

I had no time to weigh these words and their meaning. As though a hook painlessly entered my chest through my back from the rocky wall and anchored me in place, my muscles released and shoulders slumped forward. My eyes closed without my permission. Scenes played behind my lids.

"Our ancestors were friends, some were lovers." The spirit's words echoed through my mind as visions of tall, muscular women danced alongside Wild Women covered in scales, others with branches growing from their fingers and toes. Witches, laughing and partaking with the Wilds and Hunter women, wore flowered wreaths like crowns on their heads.

Another scene replaced the joyful women celebrating. Hunters, their red-hilted daggers hanging at their hips, surrounded the women. It was night, and the women's bonfire danced as they shifted from laughing to fighting for their lives. Hunter women pleaded with their brothers to stop. Some of the men paused to consider their sisters' words, but others shouted commands to push forward.

"Round them up," a Hunter sitting atop a horse shouted to the younger men on foot.

Women tried to flee into the woods in confusion, but they were surrounded.

I stood behind the waterfall, but also in the middle of a historical event I never knew happened. Unable to lift a finger to defend these innocents, I watched as they were herded nearer to the bonfire, the circle of Hunters closing in, pushing the women's backs closer to the flames.

Female Hunters urged the Wild Women and witches to be nearest the center, nearest the fire, away from the bigger threat, while they tried to reason with their brothers. Surely these men wouldn't hurt their sisters, their mothers.

Some men kept on task as tears streamed down their cheeks, while others refused to look their sisters in the eye.

The Hunter males, their black cloaks billowing in the air produced by flames, closed in on their sisters. The moment a male Hunter grabbed for a witch hiding behind a female Hunter, the female Hunter attacked her brother.

I couldn't open my eyes to pull myself from the scene playing before me, in my mind. I couldn't watch anymore. I didn't know what came next—I'd never learned about this piece of our history. But the sinking feeling in my stomach told me it wasn't good.

Suddenly, I thought to look down, away from the horror, and realized I was viewing this all from the point of view of a person involved. I was a female-bodied person, wearing brown trousers faded at the knees and a cream shift for a shirt, billowing at the arms and held in place across my chest and abdomen by a leather vest. I instinctually knew this vest was more to protect my torso from blades than for appearances.

"Huntress," a voice whispered into my mind.

My focus pulled from my garments the exact moment an arrow breezed past me, and I turned to see it slice into the neck of a Hunter. I was standing in the horde of women, witches behind us for protection, Wilds the next line of defense.

The wounded Hunter stumbled back from the blow to his neck. The Huntress he had been holding his blade to pivoted and swung out of his way as he flailed, his hands dropping the dagger to grab at the arrow. Blood pulsed and gushed down his thick neck, while the arrow remained in place.

A Wild Woman reached to the ground to steal the dagger but dropped it with a scream and jumped back. I picked the heavy blade up, a ruby in its hilt. Every second I carried the weapon, my hand ached a little more, until my fingers wrapped around the cold steel shook, their strength draining with each beat of my heart. I dropped the thing back into the dirt and eyed the others who wielded daggers.

They were all Hunters and all male. One Hunter, tears winding down his grief-twisted face, held his dagger to a Huntress's throat. Her wide eyes watched his every move with disgust and what looked like a sense of betrayal.

I had never desired to refer to myself, a female Hunter, as a Huntress, but now, the word nestled into my understanding. As if it had always been true.

I peered out over the landscape of men fighting against women for a dominion that the women never wanted. We didn't seek to control and regulate—we sought peace and health and happiness. And I suspected that was what had landed us in this position so long ago.

When Hunters and Huntresses had the same abilities, the Huntresses had a say in who the Hunter organization deemed evil and what to do about that evil.

Huntresses had refused to kill those they had befriended, and so they were stripped of their power.

I came from a long line of Huntresses.

And our brothers had turned against us. To oppress, to force submission, which is exactly how it turned out in the long run.

"Your sisters, your mother, your grandmother, they are all Huntresses," the voice said. "You have all been betrayed by your forefathers."

I couldn't know who I spoke as, the Huntress wearing the leather vest or the Huntress in sweats and a T-shirt. I only heard the question on my lips. "Why did the Hunters come here in the first place? They're not from this continent."

"You stand in Washington but view events from old Europe," the spirit answered.

"But this portal," I continued, "didn't it have other beings to keep it safe, before the witches?"

"That is another series of tragic events in history," the spirit said solemnly. "The wheel of time turns, and with it, peoples and lands shift and change as well—for good or bad. But portals do not change simply because the people change. They continue to need protection."

I couldn't say why a sudden surge of hope blossomed in my heart, but it did. "Did you bring me here to stay?" I asked. "To be with Oriana?"

I wasn't sure if spirits laughed, but I could have sworn this one did. At me.

I needed to stop thinking Oriana and I could be anything other than enemies. She wouldn't have it any other way.

"Like the humans, you are given free will, to do with your life as you please," the spirit explained. "We brought you here because you willed to know more, to know freedom from your past, and to know true love. To know your nature, your true Huntress, your deep connection to Brigid. How you move forward is solely your decision."

"I want this," I blurted, before even considering my words. "I want Oriana." It was as if my heart proclaimed my desire before my head had time to consider and evaluate. "I want to stay."

The spirit went silent. The strong presence I felt from her suddenly vanished, along with the mist.

Only Brigid's energy pinged through me now, like an electric current, amping me.

Sarah and I could be together.

I imagined her teaching yoga classes in her new structure. How I'd maintain it so she wouldn't have to think about that, so she could just concentrate on what she loved and let me concentrate on what I loved: her. And working with my hands. But mostly, I wanted to stay for her.

Yes, I'd only just met her, but I'd never met anyone like her.

The portal had its protectors—that's not why I wanted to stay. Oriana and her coven were its protectors. But to be the one that such a gorgeous and powerfully protective witch came home to...

I'd figure out the logistics later—find an apartment in town, get to know Oriana, date her, woo her.

Feelings took root that I'd only had fleeting experiences with in the past, confidence and hope and a knowing that my wants for my future were valid.

I was valid.

Who I was, a Huntress.

A woman who loved women.

And all those other parts of me that had no label, they were valid too.

Brigid smiled within me, making me feel ten feet tall.

I stepped from the rocky wall toward the roaring waterfall to touch the tips of my fingers to the back side of the powerful flow of water.

Droplets sprayed my face and coat. Everything would be okay. I was home, finally. Home within myself and home within Obsidian Falls. It had called to me, and I gladly answered.

I had to talk to Oriana, had to share with her my experience. The way I'd ran off, I needed to explain to her what had happened. I backed away from the waterfall, my toes finding purchase on the stone floor farthest from the falling water.

Carefully, I made my way from behind the back of the waterfall and down the rocky trail. Soon enough, dirt replaced stone. As I continued down the hillside, evergreens greeted me, cloaked me in darkness despite the rising of the sun behind blankets of clouds.

I couldn't wait to get back to Oriana, to have a talk, hopefully over a hot mug of coffee. I smiled just thinking about having coffee with Oriana in the coming spring months and then into summer, warmer mornings and clear nights under the stars.

I reached the bottom of the hill and headed toward Oriana's home, the waterfall's pool at my back. What other memories would we create in these woods?

I wondered if Brigid would stay with me, if she would teach me more, how to bridge the gap between what I thought I was and what I know I am.

I would find out. I couldn't wait to find out.

My footfalls felt lighter, quicker. My heart felt lighter, happier. Hope bubbled over. Finally, I had answers. I had a path, a future, a plan.

"Sarah!" Oriana's voice cut through the woods and froze my hopeful fantasies with a frigidness that iced the marrow of my bones.

I froze.

I could not see her, but I could definitely feel her, all around me, surrounding me in the woods, as if she herself was an army circling me, closing in.

"You have trespassed on this sacred land long enough, Hunter."

I stood my ground. "I'm a Huntress and have been given access to this land by the beings who know it."

If I had thought her voice was angry before, it was because I hadn't heard this one. "*I am* the beings who know this land, who protect it and its secrets from the world." Oriana's voice thundered from the evergreens, the ferns, even the ground.

The witch I imagined building a life with showed her true self, as if an invisibility spell suddenly expired. She stood ten feet from me. A cloak hung from her shoulders and closed in a straight line from her chest to the tops of her bare feet. Her hair stood from her temples, only to fall, like dark waterfalls. "Leave," she commanded. The word echoed around me in different octaves, different voices.

Icy fingers touched my back. I turned to see nothing, while the touches continued. The hairs on the back of my neck stood.

"*Get out*," Oriana shouted.

The sheer power of her voice hit me in the chest and abdomen like a sack of sand. I nearly fell backward but righted my stance, separating my feet. I lowered myself to the ground for balance.

"I'm staying," I announced. My own voice failed to reverberate from the trees. "I want to help. I want to be with you."

It didn't take magic for the witch's face, twisted in disgust, to hit me square in the heart with a piercing jab. "The only Hunter that belongs near Obsidian Falls is a dead Hunter."

"I'm a Huntress," I repeated.

Oriana shook her head. "Suit yourself."

She advanced on me inhumanly fast. With an arm thrust out in my direction, a blast of energy shoved me to the ground.

I scrambled to get back up, and did, seconds before she stood over me.

"I don't want to fight you," I said, wiping debris from my knees to try to show her I wasn't going to retaliate. "I won't fight you."

Oriana's smile wasn't one of innocent delight. It was one of dark intentions. "Fight or not," she said dryly, without so much as an ounce of warmth for me, "you will leave here or you will die here. It doesn't much matter to me."

CHAPTER TWENTY-ONE

Oriana

Huntress. I sneered the word to myself. Please. Sarah showed up pretending to be a Wild Woman, and then after she's caught, she's suddenly a Huntress? That was laughable.

I watched Sarah shift from one foot to another, as though she was preparing for me to come at her again. As though she was positioning herself. Water dripped down the shaved sides of her dark hair and wound its way down her neck.

I noticed her newly tattooed arms. Anger grew within me, a fire fueled by truth, by reality.

Won't fight me, my ass. Sarah was employing an old favorite from the Hunters' manipulation tool kit. Seem innocent, like her whole reason for existence is to help Wild Women, to protect them from themselves. From their evil natures. Hunters are only here to help. And female Hunters are weak and incapable of much.

That last part was only true because the Hunters medicated their women, literally stripping them of their abilities and strength. I was no fool. Sarah hadn't taken those meds in a long while. And she was strong. I'd seen what she could do, how she threw the two-by-fours around like they were twigs. And now that she was being questioned, she was found out, she was using another tactic of Hunters: innocence, holiness.

Sarah was trying to sell me a lie packaged as empathy.

She sucked at wrapping.

"Huntress, huh?" I asked, deciding to play her game for as long as it would take me to establish a strong connection with the plant roots beneath the soil I stood upon.

Sarah's expression shifted from confidently spewing bullshit to confidently believing I accepted that bullshit.

She smiled and looked as though she was prepared to take a step toward me but righted herself to stand in place. "Yes. We used to live alongside our brothers, fight alongside them too."

Her smile faded. She probably realized that wasn't the wisest thing to say to me at the moment.

My energetic roots reached into the dirt from the soles of my bare feet. I intended to grasp the plants' energy and draw it up through the dirt, into me. And I had been able to do just that on most of my property, but here the roots' response was weak at best.

I repositioned my footing and waited for the familiar feeling of plant energy growing roots up through me, pulsing its power into me.

Nothing.

Maybe I had an energy block.

An ounce of panic made itself known in my stomach, its heaviness growing. Once Sarah dropped the innocent Huntress act, she would advance on me. And without my connection to nature, I'd fall as quickly as a domino.

Would I take my coven down with me?

"So much has happened, Oriana," Sarah said. She placed her hands on her hips. "This waterfall is a portal." She shook her head. "Of course you know that. Your coven is here to protect it."

Yeah, and she was a Hunter standing way too close to it for my comfort. Or the comfort of my ancestors.

Duh.

I called out to my coven ancestors to help me connect to the roots of this area, these woods.

Silence.

Okay, that was unnerving.

I tried not to show my lack of support to Sarah. But I had to buy myself time before she realized my weakened state and decided to pounce.

Where were my coven ancestors? And why hadn't I thought to call my coven sisters to help? Because I had figured I wouldn't need their help. I had figured I was perfectly capable of overpowering an untrained Hunter female. But without my plant friends, there was no way I could overpower Sarah's strength.

The panic spread from my stomach like a virus, tightening my thighs and hips.

I took a few steps back and tried to reach my energetic roots into the soil again.

Sarah's smile grew.

She knew. She knew I was a sitting duck.

"I don't want to fight," Sarah said, taking a slow step toward me, eyeing me for any movement.

Goddess, I pleaded. *Help!*

Suddenly, an evergreen branch struck my peripheral vision, to my right, and I reached out to touch it. New energy flooded into my body, pulsed through my heart, and filled me with a less grounded energy, but at this point, I was a beggar and not at all picky.

I took two steps toward Sarah. Her half smile dropped.

"I have asked you to leave this place," I stated and took another step. "You refused. I then demanded that you leave." I took another step. "And still you refused. Instead"—I took a step—"you did the opposite. You came to the Obsidian Falls and—"

"It's where I belong," Sarah blurted.

I saw red. Thoughts no longer skewed my actions. I couldn't think. This Hunter was trying to claim our sacred portal. What awful things would the Hunters do if they got control over this place? They'd get a foothold and reestablish their dominion.

I ran at Sarah.

She held her arms high above her head. "I will not fight you!" she yelled.

I didn't care. I shot my arms up above my head, turning my hands in small circles to entangle air energy within my fingers and palms. Without being able to ground, the energy sputtered and spat across my skin uncontrollably.

I had meant to knock Sarah down with energy, but it refused to release in an organized stream and instead shot out in all directions from my hands. My open palms thrust against Sarah's chest, shoving her backward into the trunk of an evergreen.

"Get out!" I screeched. I shoved her backward again, past the tree. This time, she righted herself seconds before falling onto her ass. "Get away from Obsidian Falls!"

Anger boiled up from my stomach and flooded my heart. I was sick of being ignored. Tired of being used. Done with believing I was loved when I was only accepted as long as I was beneficial. Thinking they wanted me when in reality they wanted to dominate me, take what I had to give, and leave me with nothing.

"I love you, Oriana," Sarah shouted back in frustration from the ground. "Knock this crap off."

How dare she brush away my feelings and then tell me to knock it off, as though my emotions are a burden for her. "From the beginning, you've been nothing but lies."

She stood until we were just over an arm's length from one another.

I raised my arms above my head and swirled my hands to collect more air energy.

"Don't, Oriana," Sarah stated firmly. "Brigid came to me, she's with me."

I paused, my arms still above my head. It was Brigid's cross I saw on my freshly finished yoga studio. But how?

I refused to let my guard down. Hunters lie.

"Who is Brigid?" I asked, partly to trick her into revealing the lie that Brigid would have the audacity to work with a Hunter, and partly to buy myself enough time to decide what to do.

Sarah's face lit up. She stood taller. Her shoulders squared. "She's a Goddess who became a saint."

I narrowed my eyes. Anyone could know that.

Sarah must have noticed my disregard because she quickly followed up with, "The Goddesses were being silenced, snuffed out by warrior followers of a monotheistic male deity. To make sure the world wasn't left without female deities, she allowed society to demote her and saint her."

My chin lifted and my arms dropped to my side. Hunters didn't teach history that way, so Sarah couldn't have been regurgitating what she had learned growing up. In their history, it really was *his*-story. And yet Sarah spoke of a Goddess with adoration rather than condemnation. These were not the words of a Hunter.

I thought of another telling question. "Who is Brigid to you?"

Sarah smiled a smile I'd never seen before. The corners of her lips lifted, her teeth showed, her skin glowed. Even her eyes smiled. She was gorgeous. "She's my guide, she lives within me."

I gasped.

No way.

That couldn't be.

Goddesses didn't take up residence in Hunters. I'd more likely believe water and oil had magically learned to mix than take her words for truth.

"Bullshi—" I started to say before the flash of red in the distance caught my attention. The hairs on the back of my neck stood. I quieted and stilled to feel the energy around me.

All animal forest commotion, of food collecting and socializing, ceased, as though the animals in the woods suddenly disappeared.

"What?" Sarah asked, looking around behind her, clearly not worried I'd make my move against her while her back was to me.

But I wasn't that sort of fighter. And even if I was that kind of fighter, something way worse than me on a bad day watched us.

"Do you feel it?" I asked Sarah on a whisper.

She gave me a blank look. With the nearby waterfall's roar, she clearly couldn't hear my question.

I took a few steps to my left and peered out at the distance. To keep the thing from noticing I watched it back, I stared slightly more to the right than the being watching me stood, hiding itself within a cluster of thick evergreens. I couldn't see it but felt the strength of its intent, its focus directed at me.

I wanted to return to what Sarah and I were doing, get some closure for the hurt peeking through my anger, but warning bells shoved my emotions out of the way.

Tingles jolted through my arms and legs. My hands ached to gather energy, to form a sphere of protection around myself.

With all animal sounds ceased, the splattering of rain and the rustling of wind broke through the silence with an unnerving jolt. Everything in me demanded that I harness the powerful wind right away.

I threw my arms into the air and willed it as much as possible to combine with my energy and fuel me. Absorbing it was work. It felt off. The energy was…tacky, not the normal flowing existence of an element so free that it was often soundless, tasteless, scentless, and weightless. This, this was more like waving my arms through a dense yet clear fog that grabbed at my skin and smelled like rotting water.

Something mighty and old and evil was with us in these woods, and it wasn't a Hunter.

"Something's in the woods with us," I said to Sarah.

A few breaths passed before she responded, still studying our surroundings. "Should we take cover at the waterfall?"

I shook my head. "We don't want to lead it there." Unless, of course, that's where it came through in the first place. Then we'd want to either kill it or get it to go back where it came from. But Sarah wasn't a coven member. She wasn't privy to such knowledge. Outsiders couldn't know about the mysteries of the waterfall. No one could know.

Something low to the ground shimmered red and orange fifteen feet away and then disappeared before I could fully see its form.

A large fern ten feet from us, soaked from weeks of rain, burst into flames. Fire licked the air and spurted angry flecks onto the leaves around it.

Sarah shook her arms out. New black lines etched into the back of her left hand. Panic flashed in her eyes, but only for less than a second before irritation took over, along with a wince.

"Fuck, it hurts," she said in a half whine, still trying to stay alert for the threat. "Something evil is near because…"

She gritted her teeth with a sharp inhale and then opened her mouth to exhale. "My hands," she said, looking at them in awe, "they ache on the inside too." Sarah groaned and shook for a breath before steading herself again. I fought the urge to rush to her aid. "They want to wrap around something and end it," she said, still talking about her hands.

That was her Hunter. Of course. If there hadn't been some malicious-feeling being near my coven's waterfall, I would have kicked myself for wanting to help her seconds ago.

I shoved the thought away. I couldn't allow the shame to decrease my ability to work with energy in this moment.

And then another thought followed.

What could cause a Hunter and a Witch to naturally know it was an enemy of both? To make us pause our own feud to join forces against it?

A growl, low and layered, shook the ground and came from the direction of Sarah's back. She flung around in an instant and jumped to stand in front of me, facing the sound.

A black dog slunk out from behind a tree. But this was no normal dog. It stood to about the height of a miniature pony. Where ribs should be, the black molten fur opened in slits to expose liquid fire, shifting and moving, encased beneath the surface.

It lifted a black lip, its fangs sharp and extending down to reach the bottom of its jaw.

It barked with the sound of a thousand horrified screams, as though hell lived in its belly.

My body demanded I get away from this thing, get out of the woods. My town's woods. My coven's woods.

I moved from behind Sarah and steadied my stance, my cloak forming a triangle, with the top of my head, my crown chakra, directly beneath the tip of my cloak's head cover.

How could I fight such a beast without a strong connection to the nature around me? Spirit.

"Great Goddess, Mother of All, awaken my sisters for help in this moment," I muttered under my breath. "Great Goddess, Mother of All, awaken my sisters for help in this moment. Great Goddess, Mother of All, awaken my sisters for help in this moment."

Air energy pinged through me, eager for release.

The black dog sniffed the air and caught a scent. It raised its massive head, shifting the thick lava beneath its ribs. I hoped it caught a scent and would leave us be, give me time to call my coven sisters.

It flung its head and locked red eyes on the two of us. A low, nearly silent growl rumbled the ground we stood on.

The huge, fiery canine bolted straight for us.

CHAPTER TWENTY-TWO

Sarah

The evil beast lunged for Oriana. I shoved my arms through the air to block its full body blow.

Oriana screamed a sound that made my ears ring, her eyes wide and arms raised.

The beast's fur felt riddled with hot ash. It scorched my arms, yet somehow the beast recoiled from its blow to me, as though I'd neutralized it or given it a run for its money.

The beast and I worked on righting ourselves in time to crouch for another attack.

Oriana's scream, I realized, wasn't a scream at all. Her lips moved rapidly, her focus a glassy gaze trained solely on the beast.

Whose focus was solely trained on me.

Was I the distraction while Oriana worked?

So be it.

The canine huffed out a breath of smoke, watching me as though it waited for me to make a move. I stomped the toes of my boots into the dirt, establishing my place. The beast mirrored me with its front paws, claws scratching at wet soil.

I gambled by taking a quick look at my arm, the one that had connected with the beast's molten body. I shot a look back to the supernatural creature. My flesh had melted around the Hunter tattoos, as if my new ink protected the skin it etched.

"Yeah, that's gonna leave a scar," I joked before realizing I could have distracted whatever Oriana was doing and shut my mouth.

She seemed concentrated, her eyes open but not seeming to register anything, least of all the beast staring at me.

It lifted its front paws into the air and fell back to the earth with a boom that shook the ground. I crouched lower to not be thrown off-balance. The thing snorted smoke and barreled forward, right for me.

Instinctually, I turned to run and slipped in the mud, smacking my chin to the wet ground. The beast started to pull back in a zigzag move, like the thing was trying to trick me, psych me out. And then it ran forward at me before stopping abruptly and appearing to be heading in a different direction.

Was this thing playing with its food? In a panic I shoved from the mud to hop upright. I knew it was trying to throw me off, confuse me, before going in for the kill.

"Good doggy," I said low and quiet.

The idea worked and the beast paused, cocking its head. I reached my burned and quickly healing arm toward the thing, not to get it to come close for pets, but to confuse it. Because two can play at the confusion game.

In a flash swifter than it takes to form a thought, knowing settled in my stomach. I wasn't playing a game with an *animal*, supernatural or not. As if it saw my thoughts and sought to confirm them, a wave of molten lava sloshed within its eyes, two pools of bright, hot, liquid fire.

Hell lived within this intelligent, calculating being.

The hell I'd learned about growing up, pits of fire for the evilest of the evil.

Something hard hit me in the chest and knocked the air from my lungs. I coughed to catch a breath as my hands waved about, trying to keep me on my feet.

My butt hit the ground, squishing a baby fern beneath me.

Air escaped my lungs as a huge weight bore down on my chest, directly between my breasts. I tried to blink to see what was happening, my confusion growing with the smoke swirling in front of my face.

A deep burning sensation penetrated my chest, immediately followed by the familiar digging pain of a new Hunter tattoo creating itself. I knew the beast pressed a large paw into me, burning my flesh and combatting my Hunter ink, but I couldn't see the thing, its breath hot and smelling of egg and iron.

I fumbled and dug my fingers in to grab and squeeze at its thick leg, to push the paw from me so I could pull in a breath of air. When I yanked my hand away, my scorched fingers closed around what I thought was the beast's flesh. Clumps of what felt like granulated ash fell from my opened hand.

As if the beast waited for me to figure out what it already knew and wanted me to see what came next, the smoke cleared to reveal two molten eyes staring at me. Inches from my nose, it opened its mouth and bared its top set of fangs. Droplets of fiery spittle singed the skin on my face.

The beast leaned back, both its paws hovering over my chest.

Panic thudded through me. It was preparing to land the death blow.

I tore at its fur, only ending up with handfuls of sandy ash.

If it had the capacity to smile, it would have. I knew that in my bones.

It roared a sickly high-pitched sound, filling the space between us with smoke. Tiny pings of burning spit singed my skin and lit whatever plants it landed on.

I couldn't see anymore. Smoke burned my eyes. Tears rolled down my cheeks.

Its weight on me shifted, heavier in the back now, its substantial size bearing down on my thighs. It was leaning back. Preparing to strike.

And then I felt nothing. Nothing at all.

CHAPTER TWENTY-THREE

Oriana

The exact moment the last coven sister's essence arrived in the woods with us, my eyelids shot open. Over forty witches, most of them dead, circled the hell hound, Sarah, and me.

I had never seen a hell hound before, but the dead witches were certain, so I was too.

The hell hound leaned back, released a howl that sounded less like a wolf and more like women screaming, and then pounced on Sarah.

"*No,*" I yelled and shot my left arm toward the hell hound. A knobby stick shook from my clutched fist. I pulled earth energy from below and cosmic energy from above. The earth and cosmic energies met at my shoulder, combined, and picked up power until it all compacted itself into the stick and burst from its tip to the target.

The shocked hound screeched as my blast hit its shoulder, sending it tumbling off Sarah. I ran forward and pressed my knees into the mud, searching her still body for blood, a bite mark, something to indicate what was wrong, how to fix her. Her right forearm looked recently healed from a major burn and included new tattoos, but that was all.

I couldn't close my eyes to concentrate on her energetic field, to feel what was wrong with her. I kept a close eye on the hound. It lay twenty feet away, its back foot twitching. The thing was too close and too alive for my liking.

I hurriedly patted Sarah's legs, in lieu of looking down at them. Other than what felt like patches of damp cotton—I assumed collateral damage from standing so close to a waterfall—her sweats felt normal, not tacky wet from blood.

The hell hound twitched again. Good. It had been a bit long since it last moved. The last thing I wanted was a break in its pattern. Still, I watched and waited for its regular cadence of foot twitching.

My fingers patted up Sarah's waist, past the waistband of her sweats, and up her rib cage. Nothing. Then why wouldn't she wake up?

I kept patting, frantically hoping to either find the ailment or wake her in the process.

Where's the twitch? The hound went completely still. Its split ribs, lava bubbling through black bones and patchy ash flesh, rose and fell, but its leg did nothing.

"What? Mate?" Sarah yelled, jolting awake.

I gasped and pulled my hands away when I looked down and saw that they were on her breasts, patting around the seam of her sports bra.

Sarah wrapped her arms around my waist, tucked me sideways, and then spun me to be behind her. Once she placed me down, she kissed my forehead, spun again, and ran for the hell hound bolting for us.

I hurried to get up and point the stick at the hell hound again but didn't gather the energy in time, before the Hunter and the hell hound crashed into one another. Flames burst from the two bodies, flailing, fighting, and then falling.

Huntress.

Before the Huntress sacrificed herself for me.

CHAPTER TWENTY-FOUR

Sarah

My shoulder hit the beast's. I got a close-up view of its ash fur breaking away, parting, to reveal dark, pitted bones and bubbling lava. I winced when the painfully hot substance spurted from under its shoulder blade to hit my shoulder, and again, when the pain of a tattoo etching itself into me followed.

But that was just it—I was outside it all.

I was in my body, but also watching from above it.

Watching as I fell to the forest floor alongside my enemy. Watching as I jumped up, unharmed, grinning, and grabbed the beast by its neck with both hands. It fought, screeched, bubbled lava that burned holes in my clothes and skin, but I held still, smiling.

Black ink rose from any exposed skin where lava spat, my body healing the wounds directly. And yet I felt no pain, floating above myself.

I looked slightly left. Oriana stood strong, her cloak closed around her, and she pointed a stick at the beast. Dozens of witches circled the scene, their arms raised to the heavens. Wisps of what looked like color-tinted air flowed from the witches' feet and sank and rose through the soil like a water serpent, swimming through earth, until it reached Oriana's feet and disappeared.

Oriana was smaller than me, thinner than me. I'd known that, but seeing it from outside my body, seeing her stand solidly behind me as I fought, seeing her intensity…

She might have been petite, but her power exuded a strength I only wished I had. If I could choose who protected me when my back was against the wall, it would be Oriana. I ached to embrace her, thank her, promise utter devotion to her.

I loved the witch, the woman gathering a natural weapon strong enough to take out a fire beast. I didn't care that Brigid said Oriana was my mate. I *wanted* her to be my mate, deity approved or not.

As if that personal declaration was enough for me to will myself back into my body, I felt my essence jolt back to the ground, to the fighting. Only, I didn't fight alone, within my body.

A Goddess inhabited me. Brigid fought the hell hound, met its fire with a fire of her own. I knew what the beast was now because *she* knew what it was.

It felt as though Brigid came from behind me, placed her hands and arms over mine, and showed me how to use them correctly. On instinct, as the hell hound scrambled to stand after being thrown, I raced toward it.

It shook its head and opened its jaws to snap at me the moment I got close enough. I took the opening as my invitation and shoved my right arm down the beast's throat, pushing myself into it rather than away. Its eyes flashed a deep red, rather than their normal brightness of churning lava. My movement had shocked the hound.

Brigid eased backward, removing herself from the confines of my body while still guiding my movements, as though an invisible dance partner seamlessly guided my hand to ball into a fist and punch as hard as I could into the hound's throat, as far back as possible.

The beast's red eyes widened as my hand opened, grabbed, and pulled, my arm shoulder-deep.

With Brigid now completely outside my body, the searing pain returned. Melting skin, replaced by the black etching of a new Hunter tattoo, dropped me to my knees. Fire, followed by deep scratching into the raw skin.

If my body hadn't just been filled with the restorative essence of a deity like Brigid, the pain would have already knocked me out. The beast would have already ended me.

The hell hound coughed and choked as I grabbed at the burning, unprotected flesh. My fingers dove down its throat and sank into the base of its tongue. It shook its head violently to loosen my grip.

I lost my footing and shook like a rag doll in the beast's mouth.

The moment it made the mistake of lowering its head to cough, I pulled my arm from its mouth, hooked my other arm around its neck, and used its momentum to swing myself onto its back. Its ashy hide burned through my sweats and seared the backs of my thighs.

The hell hound bucked and screeched the sound of a thousand tortured screams.

The unearthly sound pierced my ears.

Visions of murder, suffering, pain, and betrayal flooded my mind with chaos. I couldn't focus. Couldn't hold the tears back, seeing and feeling such vile images.

The beast took the opportunity.

It threw itself onto its back, pinning me.

My head hit the ground with a jarring thud. The beast screeched again, releasing the sounds of hell. I instinctively tried to cover my ears, but my arms were trapped under its substantial weight. The thing twisted, as though it sought to push me deeper into the dirt. My right leg twisted and my knee popped out of socket.

Lava spilled onto me, burning through fabric and skin.

I had let my guard down for less than a second, and now I lay on the ground, helpless, beneath a huge hound of fire and molten lava.

I lifted my head to find Oriana in my line of sight and caught a partial view of her standing with legs apart. I tried to yell *I'm sorry*, but I couldn't gather enough air into my lungs to form audible words.

The pain began melting away, just like my flesh.

I supposed if I got to choose, dying as a Huntress protecting a witch would be among the most noble ways to go. Like my foremothers before me.

I had tried to send this thing back to hell. But in the end, it beat me.

CHAPTER TWENTY-FIVE

Oriana

Milliseconds ticked by as I endured Sarah's fate, as I gathered the last bits of energy needed to end this hell hound for good, as I mentally begged my coven ancestors to feed me the energy faster.

The fiery beast stood over an unconscious Sarah. Its massive front paws, black fur clinging to hanging flesh, red hot talons for claws protruding from bleeding nail beds, clung to the dirt inches from her shoulders.

It watched the slow and sputtering rise and fall of her chest. We both watched that.

Drool, slimy and black, dripped from its mouth, through a hole in its lip, dangled over Sarah's neck.

"Please," I begged.

In hazy whispers, the very last plants around us sent what little energy reserves they had left. Ferns, alderwoods, brambles all pulsed energy beneath the soil through their roots, directed at me.

The lifeblood of the soil beat faintly, entering my energetic field as though it crawled through tar to get to me. It wasn't enough.

I tried to harness it anyway, tried to concentrate the wisps of power and will the energy to exit my hand, to channel it into the stick. Willed it to strike the hell hound.

My fingers only tingled.

The beast kept its stance over Sarah, its drool loosing from its lip, hovering over Sarah's neck. She didn't move, and except for her breathing, I would think she was dead.

Panic took over. I couldn't lose her. I couldn't let this evil thing, this intruder, finish what it started. I couldn't let it win.

I called again, pleaded with the Goddess of all to help me save Sarah.

The only movement in the woods was the rise and fall of Sarah's torn and seared shirt, soaked from the rain.

The hell hound's dark saliva finally broke free from its torn lip and cut a line down the side of Sarah's neck as the acid burned through flesh.

She barely twitched in response. Had she stopped feeling pain? Was her body shutting down, giving in?

Suddenly, a new energy entered the base of my spine and shot up through my nerves, my blood, my being. Spurts of gold and green fired through my muscles, waking my chakras and aligning them for maximum potency.

Hazarding a glance away from Sarah's barely alive body under the shifting and dripping hell hound, I spied an old evergreen towering above the rest, glittering in gold and green energy. I had never seen this tree before, and yet now it was the most noticeable being in my woods.

Its power pulsed through my body. My arm shook. A stream of gold shot from the tip of my stick like a lightning bolt and pierced the hell hound. Its hellish screeches stopped, replaced by its own cries of pain.

It jerked, crushing Sarah. I didn't know if she was still breathing, but I had to do everything in my ability to save her.

She had fought off the hound, protected me, protected the waterfall.

Sarah belonged in my life, and there was no way some fire dog was going to get in the way of that.

I flicked my wrist up and the hound's torso rose off the ground, its head and legs dragging downward. It went silent as its eyes found me. The rolling lava formed into red irises and the faint trace of human fear penetrated me, made me waver.

No. It was a trick. It was trying to manipulate me into caring. I knew that feeling, I'd dealt with it more than my fair share. I hated it. Hated the way shame made me feel helpless and trapped.

"No!" I shouted.

Gold light shot from my hand.

The stick fell to my feet.

The hound's eyes flickered back to lava and then shone bright red.

I rose from the ground, hovering over pine needles and rotting leaves, righteous fury fueling me.

Gold energy spun the hound midair until it yelped and released its contracted muscles, until it gave in to my power. With a shove of my arm, the hell hound's back hit a thick, sturdy evergreen with a snap. It tumbled to the ground, listless. The molten lava beneath its torn and rotting fur ceased shifting and began to harden, slowly encasing the beast in rock.

My feet found purchase on the ground once again and I ran to assess Sarah.

She was breathing, shallow and ragged. Black ink and blood covered her skin, but no wounds. Her clothing was hanging on by threads, but the ink left her looking semiclothed.

I knelt down to her chest and placed my hands on her, my left between her breasts and my right over her belly button.

This time I channeled healing energy from the plants. They gave the blossoming green tendrils freely.

She finally twitched, and I cried in relief.

I moved my hands now to distribute healing energy to her head. Dried blood matted her short hair. She had hit her head so hard. I hoped she hadn't permanently damaged anything. And then I wondered if Hunters were able to be permanently damaged.

I caught myself wondering about Hunters and nearly laughed and then scolded myself for nearly laughing at a time like this. We were still alone in the woods. My foremothers had left, leaving only the two of us and a now dead hell hound.

I looked up from Sarah's rising and falling chest, covered in singed T-shirt and tattoos. It was done. An evil being had come through Obsidian Falls, and Sarah and I had protected the land, the town.

As if nature was validating my sense that everything would be okay, a petite fox poked her head from behind a cluster of boulders. It scampered over to us. She slowed when she reached Sarah's biceps opposite where I crouched.

"It's okay," I assured her.

She daintily stepped onto Sarah's chest and curled up, warming and covering the Huntress. I finished using plant energy to heal Sarah's head, at least enough to take a break, and removed my cloak to place on Sarah's lower half.

The fox lifted her head to watch before closing her eyes again.

"Sarah," I whispered. "You. I." The words lodged themselves in my throat. "Thank you," was all I could get out. I leaned down and pressed my lips to hers. Tears fell from my eyes and wound lines through the dirt and blood on Sarah's cheeks and neck.

Her lips opened slowly and twisted into a grin, while her eyes stayed shut. "Does this mean you like me again?"

I shook my head and laughed. "Only a Huntress would say something like that after being mauled by a hell hound."

She opened her beautiful green eyes and stared straight into mine. Her smile dropped and seriousness painted her war-torn face. "You called me Huntress."

"I'm sorry," I said. "I'll never doubt you again."

Sarah breathed out a chuckle. The fox, assured of a job well done, jumped from Sarah's chest and pranced off through the woods. Sarah rolled onto her side with a groan and pushed herself up, eyeing the little fox with a questioning gaze.

We both sat in the dirt, studying each other. "You were right to doubt me. Don't ever doubt yourself, though—that's where we slip up. When we don't believe our own reality."

I gave a nod. "So, is that some Brigid wisdom now?" I laughed.

"Brigid wisdom with Hunter tattoos. I really am a Gemini now," Sarah joked, stretching her inked arms to one side and then the other.

"Look at you!" I said too excitedly. "You know about your sign."

"I'm a Hunter, not ignorant," Sarah said, stretching her back by arching.

I opened my mouth to say they're synonymous, but she cut me off.

"Don't say it," she insisted playfully.

I looked down at her and gingerly touched her shoulder. When she didn't wince in pain, I trailed my fingers over the top of her left shoulder and up the side of her neck, dodging singe holes in her shirt.

She shivered. Heaviness filled her eyes with want.

My fingers made their way to her cheekbone. I cupped the side of her face in my hand to bring her lips to mine.

Her lips parted, and her tongue slowly found mine.

Slowly, sensually, our tongues danced.

She moaned and I pulled away. "You okay?"

She grabbed me, and before I knew it, she was on top of me, gently lowering me to the ground. "Say it again, Witch," she said, her voice heady and alluring. Hearing her call me *witch* sent tingles throughout my body.

I knew what she wanted. "Huntress," I said slowly, overaccentuating the word. As if this new word of mine had connected itself fully to the images of Sarah fighting the hell hound, the word now made my thighs ache.

Her T-shirt, torn and singed, revealed more than it concealed. Her small breasts were nearly covered in ink, like a breastplate, her own shield. Layers upon layers of Hunter patterns covered her skin until they melded together like ink blots. I doubted there was a Hunter alive as brave and strong and proven as Sarah.

My own chest warmed and tingled.

Her heart chakra connected to mine. I smiled. I had heard coven sisters talk about feeling this level of connection with another, but I'd never felt it. Now I knew. An unbreakable rope of green braided energy connected Sarah's heart to mine.

I looked up at the gorgeous, powerful woman on top of me. "Do you need to go inside and get warm?" I asked, trying to be thoughtful when all I really wanted was for her to take me.

Sarah grabbed my cloak from the ground and offered it to me. "You cold? Because I'm not."

I considered for half a second before I grabbed her face and pulled it to mine. "No," I whispered into her ear while nibbling her earlobe. "You make me hot."

She arched her back and sucked at her lower lip.

Her pelvis shifted, and I pushed mine up to grind into hers. Intensity filled her eyes with a headiness I had never witnessed before in my life. And I wanted to devour ever last morsel of her.

CHAPTER TWENTY-SIX

Sarah

Faline finished buckling Friday into her booster seat and shut the crew cab door of my truck. We had loaded everything up into the trailer, all the unused nails, screws, boards, vinyl, and fasteners, and secured it all into place. Their suitcases were in the bed of the truck, kept dry from the rain under my folding bed cover. Best investment for anyone with a truck in the rainy state.

I stood outside the truck, Oriana tucked under my arm. Together, the way we belonged.

"Congratulations on finding your tree guide, Oriana," Faline said from the front seat to the beautiful woman keeping warm by my side. She and Shawna occupied the front seats of my blue pickup, with Faline driving.

Oriana gave a nod. "I'm still in shock. I've never felt her before, and I've walked past that area more than once."

Faline smiled with knowing. "We're the children and they're the elders. When we're ready, they find us." She switched her focus to me. "So, Marcus will let you know when he finds anything out," she assured me.

Friday grinned and waved from the back seat window. I stuck my tongue out and waved back. I was going to miss that kid.

After making it back to the house last night, I had called Marcus. We talked for hours. He had never heard of Huntresses, but he was now working to track down any information on the subject. The Wild

Women said they'd check their sources as well for any old stories of us, like the ones I'd been shown in the waterfall cave.

Shawna patted the breast pocket on her flannel from the front passenger seat. "We'll get this looked at on our end too. I can't wait to see it under a microscope." Oriana had given her a piece of the cooled lava that had broken from the hell hound.

Oriana had a coven gathering planned for later that night at the waterfall and where we fought the hell hound—or as we now knew, Steven.

After the hardened lava rock cracked while transporting the beast to a coven witch's basement for study, the hell hound mystery tripled. Steven's body had been under the hardened lava.

Steven couldn't have come through the portal. He knew nothing about energy or accessing other realms. Which meant there was another hell hound who had come through and turned Steven when he came to confront Oriana. Another hell hound who actually did come from the Underworld and was likely on Oriana's property still, or at least lurking around the town of Cedarsprings.

As part of the Obsidian Falls coven's Ostara ritual, they planned to fully cleanse the Obsidian Falls waterfall and call back in the protectors of the forest. I suspected they would also brief one another and discuss the hell hound on the loose.

And most likely discuss the topic that was me and my place in all this.

With kisses blown and well wishes given, my Wild sisters and niece drove down the gravel road and out of view.

Oriana leaned her head into the crook under my arm.

"So, I was thinking," she said, as we turned and, as one unit, made our way to her little front porch and into the warm house.

"Yes?" I egged her on flirtatiously.

She pushed her shoes from her feet beside the front door. "You haven't been active in the lesbian scene, and neither have I."

"Uh-huh." I grinned and followed her.

She sat on the couch, and I stood above her, my hands running softly through her long dark hair.

"So we don't really know how to do what we want to do," she continued.

I loved when she was coy and embarrassed. I figured only I got to see that vulnerable side, and I relished it.

"I don't know," I said, "the other night we seemed to know what we were doing well enough."

She blushed. God, how I loved when she blushed.

"But I can't wait to learn it all with you," she finished.

Could she be more adorable? That was it. I picked her up off the couch and cradled her in my arms.

She laughed and pretended to beat at my chest as I carried her to the bedroom. My heart smiled, and I hoped she never stopped play-fighting with me. Never stopped blushing from my words. Never stopped leaning her head on me with a sigh.

"I will always be your safe place," I assured her.

I gently placed her on the bed, making sure to rest her head just so. I kissed her forehead and straightened to stand.

"Where are you going?" she asked, her eyes pleading.

I walked to the bedroom door to shut it, then made my way to the end of the bed and crawled across the mattress to her legs. I caressed her feet, massaging each one before spreading her legs wide for me. Her dark skirt fell from her bare knees down her thighs and bunched at her hips.

Oriana's breath hitched, and I eased my lips to her knees, brushing soft kisses along the indentation up her thigh.

Her breath caught. "What, what are you doing?" she managed to ask, as if she didn't already know where my lips were heading.

I breathed out a laugh, knowing damn well soon Oriana wouldn't have words enough to speak. "Learning."

I moved my mouth from her inner thigh back up to her left knee, gently pressing my teeth into the muscle directly above her knee, my view full of her perfection. From the highest point on her leg, my gaze traced the line along her inner thigh where muscles met and pointed to the space between her legs.

My fingers twitched to touch where my gaze rested, to push Oriana's black panties aside. Instead, I dragged my tongue along her inner thigh, finding my lips' resting place against the black fabric, soft warmth greeting my chin.

My chin moved side to side. When Oriana's exhales ended in a whine, my tongue found its way around her panties and sank into warm wetness before gliding up enough to make her shake.

I paused, my gaze meeting Oriana's. Her honey-brown eyes locked onto mine as she lovingly gazed down at me. I couldn't wait any longer to taste her. I pressed my tongue to her warmth and drew upward with it.

Oriana

Sarah's hands grabbed at my hips, pressed into the small of my arching back, as she made love to me. Her mouth worked as though she was adoring and ravenous at the same time. I tilted my hips up toward her. My hands grabbed hers when they pressed into my hips. I opened for her before the roll of pleasure cascaded through my body, my cells, along my tingling skin, up my convulsing muscles.

My legs fell to the side as Sarah kissed the inside of my thighs and rested her chin on my pubic bone. "I love you," she said.

Tears sprang to my eyes.

She crawled up my belly and rested only some of her weight on me, leaning on a tattooed arm for support. So I was lucky enough to have landed a sexy masc, tattoos and all. I nearly laughed to myself. I hadn't quite meant Hunter tattoos when I had been privately conjuring up my perfect life mate in my imagination.

"What?" Sarah asked. "Your tears and smile make me think me saying that was a good thing, but I need to actually know."

"Oh," I said on a breath. "A very good thing. Sorry." I took a breath and laughed. "I'm still tingling and a little energy-high from that." I ran my hands through her dark hair and looked right into her eyes. "I love you."

Sarah rolled onto her back with a groan. The bed shook, and I held back a laugh. This was my life now, as glorious and weird as it was.

"What does this mean now?" she asked. She propped her head up on her hand in bed beside me.

I rolled to my side to see her better. "Which part?" I asked.

"I don't live or work here," Sarah answered. "How will this work?"

This time I laughed out loud. "Babe…" I started.

"Ha!" she blurted. "That felt great."

"Good," I said. "But, babe"—I watched her smile again—"we're typical lesbians now."

She cocked her head. Clearly she didn't spend her lonely nights online, down the late-in-life lesbian rabbit hole.

I reached up to run my fingers through her hair, then trailed my hand down her neck to her shoulder and grabbed it to pull her chest onto mine. Her face hovered above mine, her breath against my lips. "It's called a long-distance relationship and then, hopefully, U-Hauling." I kissed her right cheek. "Trust me." I kissed her left cheek. "It's very lesbian."

About the Author

Rachel Sullivan is a certified peer counselor and the author of empowering stories. She lives in Washington State with her daughter and their menagerie of pets and plants.

Books Available From Bold Strokes Books

Flowers and Gemstones by Alaina Erdell. Caught between past loves and present secrets, Hannah and Vanessa must each decide if the other is worth making difficult changes for a shot at happiness. (978-1-63679-745-8)

Foul Play by Erin Kaste. Music librarian Kirsten Lindquist knows someone is stalking the symphony musicians, but can she prove that a string of murders and suspicious accidents are connected, all without becoming a victim herself? (978-1-63679-689-5)

The Hard Stuff by Ana Hartnett. When Hannah, the sales manager for a big liquor brand, moves to Alexandra's hometown and rivals her local distillery, sparks of friction and attraction fly. It turns out the liquor is the least of the hard stuff. (978-1-63679-599-7)

Hollywood Hearts by Toni Logan. What happens when an A-list actress falls for a paparazzo, having no idea her love interest is the one responsible for the photos in a troublesome tabloid scandal targeting her? (978-1-63679-695-6)

The Hunter and Her Witch by Rachel Sullivan. When an ex-witch-hunter falls for a witch, buried pasts are unearthed, and love is placed on trial. (978-1-63679-830-1)

Ride It Out by Jenna Jarvis. When the COVID-19 lockdown traps Mick and Katy in situations they'd convinced themselves were temporary, they're forced to face what they really want from their lives, and who they want to share them with. (978-1-63679-709-0)

Scarlet Love by Gun Brooke. Felicienne de Montagne is content with her hybrid flowers and greenhouses—until she finds adventurer Puck Aston on her doorstep and realizes nothing will ever be the same. (978-1-63679-721-2)

Trustfall by Patricia Evans. Devri and Shiv never expect their feelings for each other to linger, but sometimes what you've always wanted has a way of leading you to who you've always needed. (978-1-63679-705-2)

All For Her: Forbidden Romance Novellas by Gun Brooke, J.J. Hale & Aurora Rey. Explore the angst and excitement of forbidden love few would dare in this heart-stopping novella collection. (978-1-63679-713-7)

Finding Harmony by CF Frizzell. Rock star Harper Cushing has to rearrange her grandmother's future and sell the family store out from under her, but she reassesses everything because Gram's helper, Frankie, could be offering the harmony her heart has been missing. (978-1-63679-741-0)

Gaze by Kris Bryant. Love at first sight is for dreamers, but the more time Lucky and Brianna spend together, the more they realize the chemistry of a gaze can make anything possible. (978-1-63679-711-3)

Laying of Hands by Patricia Evans. The mysterious new writing instructor at camp makes Grace Waters brave enough to wonder what would happen if she dared to write her own story. (978-1-63679-782-3)

The Naked Truth by Sandy Lowe. How far are Rowan and Genevieve willing to go and how much will they risk to make their most captivating and forbidden fantasies a reality? (978-1-63679-426-6)

The Roommate by Claire Forsythe. Jess Black's boyfriend is handsome and successful. That's why it comes as a shock when she meets a woman on the train who makes her pulse race. (978-1-63679-757-1)

Seducing the Widow by Jane Walsh. Former rival debutantes have a second chance at love after fifteen years apart when a spinster persuades her ex-lover to help save her family business. (978-1-63679-747-2)

The Blessed by Anne Shade. Layla and Suri are brought together by fate to defeat the darkness threatening to tear their world apart. What they don't expect to discover is a love that might set them free. (978-1-63679-715-1)

Close to Home by Allisa Bahney. Eli Thomas has to decide if avoiding her hometown forever is worth losing the people who used to mean the most to her, especially Aracely Hernandez, the girl who got away. (978-1-63679-661-1)

Innis Harbor by Patricia Evans. When Amir Farzaneh meets and falls in love with Loch, a dark secret lurking in her past reappears, threatening the happiness she'd just started to believe could be hers. (978-1-63679-781-6)